USSR

USSR
from an original idea by Karl Marx

MARC POLONSKY
and RUSSELL TAYLOR

illustrations by Kirill Miller

faber and faber
LONDON · BOSTON

First published in 1986 by
Faber and Faber Limited
3 Queen Square London WC1N 3AU

Filmset by Wilmaset Birkenhead Wirral
Printed in Great Britain by
Redwood Burn Limited Trowbridge Wiltshire
All rights reserved

British Library Cataloguing in Publication Data

Marc Polonsky and Russell Taylor
    USSR: from an original idea by Karl Marx
    1. Soviet Union—Description and travel—1970–
    —Guide-books
    I. Title
    914.7′04854   DK29
    ISBN 0–571–13842–X

TO LEYCESTER

Contents

Introduction

What this book is *not*:

A warmonger's guide to the USSR
Fulminating catalogue of the crimes of Bolshevism as seen from the back of a CD limousine. Exposes active Soviet policy of expansionism since the Great October Socialist Calamity of 1917. Written by diplomat (ret'd), knighted for services to retarding Anglo-Soviet relations.

An apologist's guide to the USSR
Traces the development of peace-loving policies over seventy years of Soviet rule, portraying the Politburo as a misunderstood, well-meaning bunch of liberals. With its concentration on the colonialist aspirations of the US military-industrial establishment in Central America, it largely ignores the Soviet Union.

An earnest guide to the USSR
Objective, factual and very dreary account of everyday life among the Russians. Written by journalist who has lived through his three-year posting in the foreigners' enclave in Moscow, without ever setting eyes on a Russian or a rouble.

A pompous-bearded-bore-of-vague-Russian-ancestry's guide to the USSR
Book exhibiting a fascination with moribund aspects of Russian culture (opera, ballet, church architecture), interspersed with platitudinous generalizations. The fact that it is a 'personal view' justifies its total lack of contemporary relevance. Written by one of the great bit-part actors of our age.

Dullness is the best form of disinformation; the publication in this country of uniformly tedious accounts of the USSR ensures that only people whose job description precludes any sense of humour (economists, intelligence agents and Revolutionary Socialists) take any interest in the place.

What this book *is*:

Before too long (theoretically), the Soviet Union will be a truly efficient, egalitarian, Communist society. For the time being, it is bewilderingly chaotic – a hybrid lifeform requiring special survival skills and immense patience. This work is a celebration of this extraordinary society before it vanishes altogether – showing the human (i.e. sweaty, pig-headed, exasperating and endearingly incompetent) face of Socialism.

WARNING This book contains highly controversial material (e.g. portraying Soviets neither as SS-toting bogeymen, nor as lantern-jawed proletarians, but as human beings) which may prove distressing to certain individuals, e.g.:

1 *Daily Telegraph* leader writers, appalled at the omission of apoplectic rhetoric about human rights violations and Afghanistan;
2 Peace Studies lecturers, outraged by the failure to represent the USSR as a last bastion of freedom and democracy, holding out against the aggressive hegemonistic policies of Reagan and Thatcher.

Less ideologically-polarized and less humourless members of the human race may find this book entertaining and informative.

Note to feminists
Throughout the text, where the gender of a character is not specified, the male pronoun has been employed. Readers who feel that this constitutes a violation of women's rights should address themselves to the authors, who will be happy to send personalized non-sexist abuse by return of post.

Note to Oppressed National Minorities in the Soviet Union
We have given in to the convention of using 'Russians' to denote all the peoples of the Soviet Union, regardless of which of the 100 ethnic groups they actually belong to. We apologize to all non-Russian Soviets for this vicious slur, and realize that in the USSR the price for committing this simple ethnographic confusion is a broken head.

Note on currency
1 rouble = 100 kopecks
For the convenience of readers of this book, the British Government has, over recent years, allowed the pound to plummet to approximate parity with the rouble.

Note to pedants
Dates in the Julian Calendar (Old Style), designated by the letters OS, are twelve days behind dates in the Gregorian Calendar (New Style), adopted after 1917.

To assist readers unfamiliar with this convention, no such dates are included in this book.

PART ONE

1 · Arrival

Your first visit to the Soviet Union is destined to be a fairly bewildering experience. It is not at all like going to Europe, where, though they can't speak English and the food's terribly greasy, at least they share the same fundamental values as us (i.e. they eat McDonalds and wear Frankie Goes to Hollywood T-shirts).

The *First Proletarian State in the World* is structured along radically different lines – it has reached an advanced stage of the general revolutionary process, as dictated by the objective laws of history, and attained through a Marxist–Leninist implementation of the basic methodology of *Scientific Communism*.* It challenges concepts which we in the West believe to be fundamental: liberal pluralism, democratic humanism and getting your own way.

To help you acclimatize to this radical new order, Sheremetevo-2, Moscow's international airport, is a consoling compromise between East and West – a rare instance of economic cooperation across the Iron Curtain, combining the very best of homegrown and foreign expertise. For example, the high technology (X-ray scanning machines, conveyor belts, etc.) comes by courtesy of Phillips and other top-name Western firms, while the USSR lays on services in areas in which *it* undoubtedly leads the world (petty officialdom, bureaucratic obstructionism).

Excited by the prospect of this stimulating new experience, you stride energetically down strangely-deserted neon-lit chrome-and-

---

* *Scientific Communism*   The study of the general revolutionary process, based on the following principles:

1 common ownership of the means of production and equal participation in the production process;
2 transformation of the material, spiritual and economic relations within society itself, in line with the scientific-technical revolution;
3 other extremely boring things.

glass corridors towards Immigration, passing only the occasional po-faced sentry. Suddenly you round a corner and encounter your first Soviet queue – the tailback from passport control.

This queue acts as an informal quarantine, forcing you to wait around in the arrivals hall for forty minutes. The delay gives you an opportunity to study the unfamiliar elements in your surroundings.

Arrivals board   This reads like a rollcall of the principal cities of Progressive Humanity, with flights, unavoidably detained by adverse weather conditions, from Ulan Bator, Maputo and Ho Chi Minh City.

Personnel   All the airport employees seem to be working on an official go-slow. This is not some kind of industrial action (strikes are not necessary under the Dictatorship of the Proletariat), but the normal state of affairs. In the West, we rush everywhere, never stopping. This constant activity has many detrimental effects: high incidence of cardio-vascular disease, stress-related disorders, efficiency, etc. In the Soviet Union, everything proceeds at a healthier pace – one tenth of normal human speed.

IMMIGRATION FORMALITIES

So as not to throw you in at the deep end, normal Soviet procedure is slightly compromised. At both passport control and customs, you are accorded a degree of *personal service*. Make the most of it: this is the only occasion during your stay that any concession will be made to the Western notion of the *individual*.

Passport control

This is designed to root out CIA infiltrators and drive everyone else to distraction. Each passenger in turn stands and suffers the impassive scrutiny of a fresh-faced soldier, who appears to be about fourteen, sitting in a glass box.

You are immediately impressed by the iron discipline of the Soviet Army, as the soldier does not so much as smile on seeing your passport photograph. Instead, for a full ten minutes, his blank stare focuses alternately on your documents or on some detail of your physiognomy.

Irritated by the boy's insolence, you try to outstare him, but immediately feel this makes you look suspicious. Quickly you change your tactic and try to act at ease: putting your hands in your pockets; glancing casually around the room; whistling selections from Gilbert and Sullivan, etc. Still his inscrutable gaze bores through you. You squirm abjectly. You are overcome with a feeling of utter wretchedness. Your whole soul is overwhelmed with the desire to confess to some heinous crime against the Soviet state.

To prolong your embarrassment, the soldier now puts into play the following ploys:

1 he tests suspected counter-intelligence agents for extreme stupidity by asking trick questions (e.g. pointing to your passport photo and saying 'Is this you?');
2 without lowering his gaze from your eyes, he picks up a telephone receiver and speaks urgently into it;
3 he is joined by an identical 14-year-old, who also stares at you.

At this stage even the most resilient undercover agent breaks down out of sheer boredom; passengers of nervous disposition spontaneously confess to anti-Soviet outrages; everyone else is allowed to proceed through to baggage reclaim.

Customs

British customs pays lip service to the notion of 'innocent until proven guilty'. Incoming passengers are allowed to judge for themselves whether they have anything to declare at customs and walk through the appropriate channel. This enlightened system has traditionally protected the right of illegal immigrants to lug suitcases of hashish through the green channel past crowds of nattering customs officers.

In the Soviet Union, *all* arriving guests are presumed guilty of gross violations of Customs and Excise regulations and must wait in line to be examined by inspectors.

In the grip of false and highly discriminatory preconceptions about 'the gentle sex', you will probably elect to be processed by one of the female customs staff. This is a bad mistake. The Soviet Constitution grants women the full and unconditional right to be every bit as officious and vindictive as men, and your official has a keen awareness of her democratic entitlements. Noting that you appear a little flustered after your ordeal at passport control, she will immediately single you out for the privilege of having your luggage publicly dismantled.

As you lay your belongings out like a white elephant stall beneath her stern proletarian gaze, you become a little ashamed of the bourgeois trappings you have brought with you. Anticipating conditions of antediluvian barbarism, you have packed soft toilet paper, jars of instant coffee, Mars bars, etc. However, her gaze is not so much scornful as thoughtful, as she wonders which of these desirable items she can contrive to impound on some pretext. Unfortunately, toilet paper does not fulfil any of the requisite conditions for confiscation, as it is not by nature *political* or *religious*, and only by a great stretch of the imagination *pornographic*.

At this point she abruptly loses interest in you and motions impatiently at you to repack your suitcase. Her look seems to rebuke you for leaving your belongings lying about so carelessly, and for so brazenly flaunting your bourgeois affluence.

To the great gratification of your fellow passengers and customs officers alike, you now find that you can't fit everything back into your suitcase. As you bundle your clothing into it and struggle to zip it up, you strongly suspect that the official has added extra items to the collection out of malice. However, your one thought is to quit this arena of humiliation, so you stuff surplus objects into your pockets and drag your suitcase away with carelessly-repacked clothing bulging haphazardly out of it.

In this weakened and degraded state, you stumble through the airport's automatic doors – straight into the arms of Soviet reality . . .

2 · Accommodation

ARRIVAL AT YOUR HOTEL

Intourist (Moscow) Ltd, the State Travel Organization, keep you in complete ignorance of all details of your holiday arrangements. You have no idea which hotel you are staying in until you are turfed out of your tourist bus in front of it.

Wherever you are staying, you will remark upon the indifference with which you are met. The efficient running of a Soviet hotel precludes any pandering to individuals.* The *porters* watch nonchalantly as you lug your baggage from the coach. The *woman at reception* will not even bother to look up at you as you approach. She simply takes your passport and begins the mammoth bureaucratic formality of registration.

While she transfers all the details of your citizenship and date of birth into a voluminous register, performing heroic feats of procrastination by copying everything out in laborious long hand, you will have ample opportunity to learn your surroundings by heart.

You will be struck by the profusion of *tourist groups* in the hotel lobby. Out of a Marxist-Leninist belief in the supremacy of the mass over the individual, the Soviet Tourist Industry does not like to deal with humanity unless it is packaged together into neat, docile units of thirty or more. So the ground floor of the hotel will be crammed with tour parties from all over the globe, come to pay tribute to the Leading Country of the Socialist World. These consist of:

1 curious or ideologically impressionable Westerners;
2 visitors from the fifteen Soviet Socialist Republics, most of which you've never heard of;

* Unless the individual has any clout in Soviet society.

3 tourists from Fraternal and Progressive nations,* not currently in the throes of internecine combat, drought or epidemic.

This diversity leads to difficulties with awkward combinations of nationals who find one another repulsive (ethnically, ideologically or otherwise). In the interest of reducing tension between hostile groups, the classless society that is the Soviet Union has been forced to introduce three categories of hotel.

Deluxe class

Identifying features The architectural highlights of Soviet cities: huge, stirring, upwardly-mobile highrise blocks – named in honour of some appropriately vast and sprawling entity (Cosmos, Russia). Built by cheapskate West European contractors modifying existing designs for multi-storey car parks and airport terminals.

Facilities

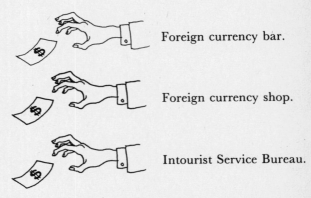

Foreign currency bar.

Foreign currency shop.

Intourist Service Bureau.

Notes It is very probable that you will be despatched here, as these hotels have been specially designed to facilitate the extraction of *hard currency*† from foreigners. In the interests of this noble aim, a limited restoration of bourgeois values has been tolerated: marble colonnaded lobbies, full mod cons, politeness of staff, etc. Awesome

---

* *Fraternal nation* One whose people have embraced Marxism-Leninism.
Progressive nation One whose people, while not having actually embraced Marxism-Leninism, at least have not yet sold out to capitalism – usually because they are still toying with some form of feudalism.
† *Hard currency* The currency of any country which is neither Fraternal nor Progressive. Consequently, it is quoted on international exchange markets and is of some value.

specifications are fixed at: 22 storeys, 1247 rooms, 2501 beds, restaurant seating 2350.

First class

Identifying features   Smaller, traditional hotels with exotic names that conjure up old world elegance (Metropole, Astoria). Quaint pre-revolutionary features (e.g. sanitation) have been fully preserved.

Facilities

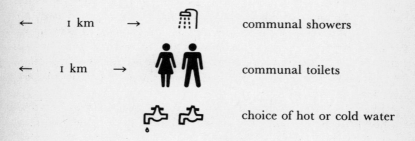

← 1 km →	communal showers
← 1 km →	communal toilets
	choice of hot or cold water

Notes   As tourists are allotted accommodation according to the buying power of their currency, you are unlikely to be billeted on anything much worse than this, pending a radical shift in the value of the pound against the Yemeni jihad.

Besides Westerners, the clientele is recruited from tourists from the more affluent Brother Socialist countries (e.g. German Democratic Republic) in the hope that the provision of a few creature comforts will help take their minds off Reunification.

Third class

Identifying features   Extremely unsavoury hotels, optimistically named after a region which, while within the borders of the Soviet Union, is close enough to the European frontiers to convey an impression of quality and hygiene. (e.g. Karelia, Baltic).

Facilities   NONE.

Notes   Accommodation here is generally reserved for organized groups of Bulgarians and squads of young Estonian gymnasts on tour. However, if you have signed up on a 'budget' holiday, or if you get caught up in the repercussions of a diplomatic incident, you will have the privilege of being billeted here.

As such hotels are generally oversubscribed, there are sometimes four people to a room, except in the case of married couples where there is a maximum of three.

GETTING TO YOUR FLOOR: THE LIFTS

The hotel management goes to great lengths to provide alternative methods of health care for its clientele. With refreshing simplicity they have found that, instead of state money being frittered away on swimming pools and saunas, the most effective way of keeping in trim is a brisk canter up and down the emergency stairs several times a day. To encourage guests to take their daily constitutional, the management ensures that only two out of the eight lifts are working at any given time.

Bear this in mind at supper-time. When you and two hundred others stream out of the dining room after the first sitting, you may choose to walk off your dinner rather than take up fruitless vigil outside the lifts.

THE DEZHURNAYA (FLOOR SUPERVISOR)

One of the dire consequences of full employment is that vicious old ladies are wheeled out of retirement homes and set loose on a corridor of terrified guests. Stationed by the lifts on your floor, the *dezhurnaya* is responsible for:

1 Your welfare and comfort, helping you to acclimatize to the atmosphere twenty storeys above ground level.
2 Your personal conduct, hygiene and morality. Note that she is bound to report to the management if there are moans, thrashings of whips or sounds of religious devotion emanating from your room.
3 Providing guests with tea in their rooms. She will discharge this duty especially assiduously if she suspects that any of the above anti-Soviet outrages are being perpetrated within.

Her domain is a small hall, like a sitting room, furnished with sofas, armchairs and a permanently-on television. This area doubles up as a departure lounge for guests wishing to use the lift service.

Here you may relax, drink tea and strike up fraternal conversation with your Vietnamese neighbours while your flight to ground level is indefinitely delayed for technical reasons.

YOUR ROOM

Though miserable pen-pushing non-entities back home, certain tourists are convinced that their very presence in the Soviet Union represents a grave threat to state security, and that they have consequently been placed under round-the-clock KGB surveillance. This type, on entering his hotel room, will spend the first ten minutes searching in tense silence for listening devices. To flatter such guests' egos, the hotel management has equipped rooms with a range of sinister and suspicious fittings (smoke detectors, TV aerial sockets, coat pegs, etc.) which very stupid people may knowledgeably identify as sophisticated surveillance equipment. Eventually one of these items will be discovered by the self-appointed Smiley with a stifled cry of triumph. For the remainder of the trip he will conduct his social life under the shower.

To the less romantically minded, Soviet hotel rooms seem fairly familiar, Socialist Man still retaining most of the bodily needs of his bourgeois cousin. The only object which may cause some puzzlement is the *radio set*. Intriguingly this device has no 'off' switch, so, short of pre-emptive violence, the best you can do to disable it is to turn the volume down to a whisper. This, of course, does not prevent it from planting subversive autosuggestions in your brain while you are sleeping.

YOUR BATHROOM

Shower The simple provision of a shower curtain is not deemed a sufficient precaution against the potential violence of the guest's ablutions. Instead, the whole bathroom is a sort of padded cell for deranged bathers, with tiled walls and a large plug-hole in the middle of the floor; the clear assumption being that anyone taking a shower is mentally unstable and likely to throw a huge violent fit and spray the room with water.

Toilet The Soviet toilet bowl is equipped with a low shelf which allows the user to inspect his excreta before flushing them away. Far from being repulsive and debased, this daily routine is actually rather fascinating, allowing one to observe one aspect of life in the Soviet Union which is truly more variegated and colourful than its Western equivalent.

HOTEL FACILITIES

Currency exchange

This is where your dollars and pounds are exchanged for Mickey Mouse roubles. In the West, any financial transaction so blatantly one-sided would arouse the interest of the Fair Trading Commission. You queue for twenty minutes, go through a flurry of form-filling, present a crisp wad of ten-pound notes and are handed a miserable clump of roubles whose shrunken size is indicative of their buying power. You may well conclude that the official exchange rate is one of the most profitable State rackets in the USSR. Do not be alarmed at the glazed look in the cashier's eyes. This is a quite normal state of catatonic withdrawal, induced by the daily handling of a king's ransom in hard currency.

Intourist Service Bureau

This body is responsible for assailing you from the moment you enter the hotel with propositions of additional excursions payable in vast sums of hard currency. Under no circumstances can they be enjoined to accept Soviet money.* This shamelessly eager pillaging of your dollars and pounds doubtless proceeds from the most revolutionary of motives: to hasten the collapse of capital and effect a more just distribution of wealth. But it is disconcerting to find that your disdain for the rouble is shared by the Soviet Government Treasury.

In fact, the Intourist Service Bureau operates as a conversion course into Socialist norms. When you arrive in the USSR, you are still firmly in the grip of your capitalist conditioning, clinging to two

---

* Though Intourist employees, like all other Soviets, are immensely proud of their Motherland and its achievements, they do not allow patriotism to cloud their better judgement in financial matters. A strict policy operates that all payments to them must be made in *convertible* currency.

26

notions essential for survival in the bourgeois world: *individuality* and *money*. The hotel registration, by confiscating your passport and forcing you to submerge your identity in that of the group, has freed you of the first. The Intourist Service Bureau is determined to rid you of as much as possible of the second.

As it happens, most of the excursions they offer you (visit to the Botanical Gardens, tour of the Metro) could be more agreeably done on your own, for a minimal outlay of kopecks and initiative. The Service Bureau has been invented as a way of giving you *even less* for your hard currency than the official exchange rate.

Post Office

The hotel has its own post office, with daily collections of residents' letters. The only difference between this establishment and its English equivalent is that the Commission for State Security seems to regard the post box as a suggestions box and eagerly scours all items placed in it for constructive (or otherwise) criticism of the Soviet regime. Bearing in mind that all your intimate correspondence to your loved ones back home is destined to become something of an open letter, to be relished by the intelligence staff of both countries, you are advised to refrain from embarrassing endearments or subjective speculation..

VENTURING OUT OF THE HOTEL

The more self-important tourist flatters himself on his Sherlock Holmes-like abilities to scent out and expose shortcomings in Soviet society. So he is convinced that every time he wanders out on his own he is being followed by a whole division of KGB officers. He spends the whole evening scurrying down side-streets, hurriedly changing Underground trains and doubling back on himself in a determined effort to shake off his tail.

The only effect of this, of course, is to get hopelessly lost. Obtaining directions from passers-by in the USSR is not as easy as it is elsewhere for an English-speaking tourist. As the USSR has never had the honour of being a British colony or screening an American soap opera, most of its subjects remain stubbornly ignorant of the First Language of Capitalism. Naturally, you are scarcely justified in feeling aggrieved at this state of affairs, as you display an even bigger (and pigger) ignorance of their language.

The result is that, as you are whisked out towards the Zheleznodorogy suburb by rapid trolleybus, you may begin to wish that the Internal Security Forces had indeed kept a close watch on your movements.

GETTING BACK INTO THE HOTEL

Getting back to the hotel is only half the battle; you still have to get *in*. This involves negotiating the *doorman*.

First-time visitors to the USSR should quickly rid themselves of all notions of the passive lackey who touches his cap respectfully as you pass. The Soviet doorman's function is less ceremonial. The hotel, packed as it is with Westerners, their values and their commodities, has great appeal to the more shady members of society, and the doorman is constantly on the look-out for Soviets trying to infiltrate this bastion of the bourgeoisie.

To this end he turns the hotel entrance into a Checkpoint Charlie, stopping all comers and demanding immediate production of their *kartochka* (hotel resident's card). Should you mislay this crucial identity document you are stripped of your Western status and become almost as contemptible in his eyes as a Soviet citizen. In this event he may avail himself of a host of emergency powers which authorize him to:

1 prevent registered guests from entering, pending production of requisite piece of grubby cardboard from deep in trouser pocket;
2 frogmarch reluctant or suspicious guests to hotel administration for positive security vetting;
3 make sweeping generalizations about guest's country's Second World War effort.

Regular off-duty reading of *Voennaya Pravda** editorials has bolstered up his indignation at free-thinking and debauchery and this will be vented should you try to get into the hotel after midnight. He will expound his misgivings about Western decadence in angry mime through the locked glass door while you freeze out on the street.

* *Voennaya Pravda* 'War Pravda' – military review which hankers nostalgically after the disciplines and privations of the 1940s.

BEDTIME

After the trauma of gaining access to the hotel, you are just about ready to put an end to your first day in the Soviet Union. Even the prospect of squirting water all over your bathroom cannot tempt you, and you make straight for your bed . . . where you uncover one last surprise.

When the Soviets make a bed they make what we in the West would term an 'apple-pie bed'. You will find that the chambermaid has neatly folded the sheets, placed them in a pile and covered them with the bedspread. This ensures that the bed must be re-made by the guest before it can actually be slept in.

At the end of a long day you may fail to appreciate this stirring evidence that the spirit of revolutionary subversion has not been entirely lost in the domestic service.

3 · Tourists' obligations

A purposeful Marxist–Leninist society has no time for the tiresome phenomenon of foreigners roaming around at random, pestering natives with their inane observations and inquiries. Intourist insists that all stray tourists are rounded up and placed under the strict supervision of a *guide*, who remains with the group throughout its stay in the USSR.

The guide's job-description incorporates *three* basic functions:

Disciplinarian   He is the drill sergeant entrusted with the task of transforming a woolly group of individualists into a crack corps, able to withstand daily exposure to war museums and Armenian folk concerts. To this end he instils a strict and binding obedience to the *Itinerary* – the immutable code of law imposed by the Soviet Tourist Board. An extremely dim view is taken of maverick tourists wishing to secede from the collective or questioning the desirability of the day's required excursions.

Ideologico-educational   The buffer zone between you and Soviet reality, the guide is responsible for interpreting your surroundings to you. Shielding you from aspects of public life which you are liable to misconstrue (queues in shops, manifestations of Party privilege, etc.), he offers reassuring explanations for other temporary imperfections in Soviet society.

Liaison   The guide is the tourists' link with the authorities, and will not hesitate to offer a helpful tip-off to the powers that be should any of his charges be suffering from adaptational problems (visiting refuseniks, selling jeans on the black market, etc.).

Soviet guides are horrified by the Westerner's slipshod approach to sightseeing. To Soviet eyes the foreigner's preferred method – simply wandering around looking at things – is laughably reactionary and narrow-minded. How can one derive any satisfaction from, say, St Isaac's Cathedral without knowing its height, cubic capacity and the number of Tsarist serfs who perished during its construction?

By contrast, in the USSR, *Scientific Tourism* is a strict discipline, instilled into children from an early age. Like other Soviet sciences, it is:

Objective and verifiable   Eschewing the narrow subjective standard of 'beauty',* it is concerned only with indisputable, provable facts (dates, weights and measurements, etc.).

Progressive   The guide is rather rankled by Westerners' aesthetic posturings and preoccupation with Tsarist follies (the Winter Palace, St Basil's Cathedral, etc.). Scientific Tourism demands that an equally high profile be given to *Soviet* contributions to the city skyline: towering new microregions, television factories, Palaces of Culture, etc.

Exhaustive   Reluctant to discriminate against other buildings merely because they lack imagination in design and construction, a general amnesty is declared. This leads to the rehabilitation of most remaining structures on the grounds that, whatever their aesthetic failings, they are at least *Soviet*. So it is that even extremely ugly buildings turn out to be miracles of post-war reconstructionism.

There is a certain advantage to this system. After all, one of the most regrettable things about our so rashly accorded 'freedom of speech' is that it gives any pig-ignorant clod the inalienable right to sound off in public on subjects he knows nothing about. In the Soviet Union citizens are absolved from the burden of making aesthetic judgements: after all, they do not have the qualifications. Instead, they maintain an obedient silence and listen to the guide, who, with all the relevant hectares and metric tonnes at his fingertips, is entrusted with formulating all subjective opinions on their behalf.

THE ITINERARY

Intourist has an enlightened approach to visitors from foreign shores. It does not kowtow to them in recognition of the fact that their dollars

---

* It would be inappropriate to use beauty as a standard in the Soviet Union, because it is:
(*a*) subjective, unscientific and imperialistic by nature;
(*b*) relatively rare.

are propping up a decrepit economy, as we do in Britain. Instead you will be treated with an impressive indifference. Your guide will inform you of last-minute changes to your itinerary – Intourist having decided that instead of the churches and priceless art collections of Leningrad, you would rather marvel at the Palace of Sport and the Headquarters of the Regional Soviet in Kalinin.

Wherever you end up, you will be broken in on your first morning with a gruelling three-hour *sightseeing tour of the town*. In places of genuine interest (e.g. Hero-Cities Moscow and Leningrad*), this is quite an agreeable interlude. In provincial holes (where Intourist has kindly arranged for you a four-day surprise stop-over), you may spend the time circling Victory Square over and over again, allowing you to take photographs from all conceivable angles . . .

This excursion will normally be conducted by a *local guide*, in whom a lifetime's enforced abstinence from twentieth-century culture has instilled a deep love for his own little backwater. His panegyric monologue will reveal his two other loves.

Uniformity   He will fondly list the aspects of his town which make it exactly the same as all other Soviet cities, e.g.:

- it is a Major Industrial and Cultural Centre;
- it is renowned for its wide avenues and flower-filled parks;
- its people are distinguished by their love of singing and dancing.

Facts   The guide has a statistic for every occasion and willingly satisfies tourists' curiosity on a wide range of topics: principal industrial products, annual production norms, water consumption per capita, etc. For those of a more frivolous disposition, he will also answer questions on the arts, fortifying his city's suspect claims to cultural sophistication by stressing the extremely high quantity of its theatres, museums and Institutes of Higher Education.

So as not to shatter this fragile industrio-economic overview of the city, the guide is reluctant to allow his charges to leave their tourist bus except to make a closer inspection of monuments to local revolutionary figures.

* *Hero-City*   Honorary status given to certain cities for fortitude in the struggle against Hitlerite Fascist invaders during the Great Patriotic War (see footnote page 35).

MUSEUMS

Hero-City Minsk is the Soviet tour guide's dream town, as the place has been razed to the ground on so many occasions that no building more than forty years old remains standing. With no architectural distractions and minimal exposure to reality, the guide may lead you directly to the first museum.

Guides like the order and compactness of the museum, where everything is well laid-out, unambiguously labelled and neatly contained behind glass panels – in pleasant contrast to the sprawling chaos on the street outside. Where the *practice* may leave a little to be desired, the *theory* of Soviet life (as displayed in the Museum of the Great October Socialist Revolution and the Exhibition of Economic Achievements) is bound to fill the citizenry with pride and hope for the future.

How to behave in a museum

Intourist feels that, like most other aspects of the human experience, a visit to a museum cannot be fully appreciated without a sustained and detailed commentary on its various ideological ramifications. To this end, all visitors are shunted off on a *guided tour*.

At a pace adapted to suit any octogenarians in the group, the guide proceeds methodically through the museum, coming to a standstill in front of each display to deliver a clipped narrative in a polished monotone. Each explanation lasts precisely ninety seconds, as it is considered inegalitarian to linger less over one exhibit than over any other.

Group solidarity of this kind does not suit the British, who fail to be moved by mention of the Leading Role played by the Communist Party in relation to each exhibit. Many guides taking round a group of Westerners find, at the end of the museum, that their hour-long monologue has in fact been a soliloquy.

To discourage sloping off on one's own, in every room there is stationed a *supervisor* – a woman of middle years dressed (doubtless because she feels so at home in her work) in informal attire of apron and slippers. It is her responsibility to thwart any loitering with intent to break away from the group. Any individuals demonstrating the inherently expansionistic nature of their imperialist heritage are met with a strict policy of containment.

33

SOME MUSEUMS

Though he will preside over the entrance halls to the majority of museums in the form of a large statue or oil painting, V.I. Lenin has one museum all of his own, to which you will be invited to pay homage.

Museum of V. I. Lenin

V. I. Lenin travelled extensively through Russia during his lifetime, and just about every town where he made so much as an overnight stop has seen fit to honour the occasion by setting up a Museum of V. I. Lenin. Towns not actually visited by the Great Statesman often console their grief-stricken population by setting up a Museum of V. I. Lenin anyway. Such exhibitions will proudly flaunt any tenuous affiliation with the Great Leader (e.g. featuring blow-ups of the footnote to *Marxism on the State* in which he calls on the local proletariat to get their act together, displaying models of the house in the area where his aunt lived, etc.).

Though photographs of V. I. Lenin, with and without hairpiece, are numerous, they tend to reveal a side of the man that the authorities would rather play down for ideological reasons – that he was unashamedly cute and quite incapable of looking stern. Photos are carefully supplemented with some suitably severe statues and paintings, depicting V. I. Lenin with a brow and lower lip more befitting the Founder of the First Socialist State in the World.

Bona fide memorabilia of V. I. Lenin are generally a bit thin on the ground. If you trudge out to the desolate wastes of the Gulf of Finland, you can see a *shalash* (straw wigwam) very like the one in which Vladimir Ilytch once crashed out. The House-Museum of V. I. Lenin in V. I. Leningrad itself actually possesses a genuine cushion, as sat on by the Great Practician, amid an extensive collection of non-authentic relics. Less fortunate museums must make do with blatant fakes: e.g. an overcoat with some holes in it, resembling the one V. I. Lenin was wearing when shot in 1918.

Detailed treatment of the *Great October Socialist Revolution* is avoided because:

1 most of V. I. Lenin's pronouncements on Marxist doctrine are generally deemed so dry as to be unpalatable even to the Soviets;
2 thanks to the tireless efforts of J. V. Stalin, most leading participants in the Bolshevik revolution were later exposed as hostile

agents of imperialism, who had, in fact, been constantly working to subvert the revolutionary cause in Russia.

As a result, the displays feature, in the main, lots and lots of photographs of the same lowly and uncontroversial revolutionary understudies (F. M. Mantulin, P. A. Dzhaparidze) through the years. This means that the exhibition is principally of value to students of political science with a special interest in the development of Y. M. Sverdlov's facial hair during the First Russian Revolution (1905–7).

Sometimes the authorities find that they have overestimated, and the four-storey palace they had ambitiously commissioned to house the museum proves far too large for the paltry number of available artefacts and documents relating to the Great Lenin. In such cases, despite the fact that the man himself died in 1924, the management judges it not inappropriate to dedicate whole halls of his museum to the history of the Great Patriotic War* and, further on in increasing desperation, to photographs of M. S. Gorbachev visiting an oil refinery in Krasnodar and models of the Soviet cruise ship *Leonid Brezhnev*.

Mausoleum of V. I. Lenin

If you wish to pay a personal call on Uncle Ilytch, you will find him in his mausoleum outside the Kremlin most weekdays (9–5). Fittingly, the Father of Proletarian Internationalism can command the mightiest queue in the whole of the Land of the Soviets: it straggles around Red Square, past the Eternal Flame and off into the distance. Privileged Westerners, however, usually get to barge in half-way along, which means that they eventually arrive at the mausoleum with only a mild case of frostbite. Filtering respectfully past the guard of honour, you pass into the sepulchre, and gaze upon V. I. Lenin himself, who lies embalmed in a ceremonial bed. Besides wondering why he was wearing a suit in bed, you are struck immediately by the fact that the man was a midget.

Certain sceptical tourists, after viewing the exhibit, have suggested that the Great Thinker might have been commissioned from Madame Tussaud's. Regrettably the authors must scotch such

* This event, with the addition of a few minor skirmishes in Western Europe, North Africa, Asia and the Pacific is better commemorated elsewhere as *World War Two*.

fanciful speculation. Were it the case that Our Friend and Teacher was a waxwork, it is certain that the over-reverential Soviet sculptors responsible would have endowed him with a six-foot frame, square jaw and barrel chest.

House-Museum of the Obscure Cultural Figure

Though Moscow and Leningrad own the exclusive rights to Figures you might actually have heard of (e.g. Tolstoy, Chekhov, Tchaikovsky), the more out of the way Industrial and Cultural Centres have been encouraged to put forward their own contenders, who have bolstered the local contribution to world artistic heritage.

Sifting through the mass of items which fell under its aegis after the Great October Socialist Revolution, the Soviet Ministry of Culture has unearthed traces of many poets and painters who have not troubled posterity anywhere else in the world. This cherished inheritance of memorabilia (pen-nibs, pallets, tea services) is put on display in the Figure's former residence, where he lived intermittently between 1852 and 1853. Those immortalized in this way include *D. I. Guliya*, who translated Pushkin and Shakespeare into Abkhazian, and *K. L. Khetagurov* (1859–1906), the 'Leonardo da Vinci of North Ossetia'.

Soviet observers can usually detect, in the cosy landscapes or laudatory odes to rural life, stirring evidence of proto-Bolshevik sympathies, especially in those Figures who lived long before Socialism was invented.

In regions whose annals boast no Cultural Figure whatsoever, the shortfall has been resolved by assigning to the under-represented area another Cultural Figure – drawn from a pool of unclaimed genii of no fixed nationality. In this way, *Omar Khayyam* has been bloodlessly annexed and proclaimed a great national hero of Soviet Uzbekistan and the Father of Uzbek Literature.

Museum of the Obscure Revolutionary Activist

Any local contribution to the general revolutionary process, however paltry, is eagerly seized upon by the Regional Party Organization and commemorated in a Museum of the Obscure Revolutionary Activist. These Revolutionary Activists vary considerably in stature – from the relatively obscure (e.g. *G. K. Ordzhonikidze*, People's Secretary of the Transcaucasus Executive Committee, 1921–6) to the practically-unheard-of (e.g. *J. V. Stalin*, whose name is rarely mentioned in the Soviet Union outside his native Georgia).

The museum is housed in the local building with the highest revolutionary credentials:

- the hall in which the first Soviet of Workers' and Soldiers' Deputies was triumphantly convened in 1917;
- the basement in which the Russian Social-Democratic Labour Party (Bolshevik) published its underground newspaper before the First Bourgeois-Democratic Revolution in 1905;
- the front room where a few vague utopians rebelling against their parents sat round reading each other mistranslated foreign monographs in the late 1880s.

Special exhibitions are devoted to issues of particularly vital concern in the locality. For example, the House-Museum of the Eminent Professional Revolutionary Alexander Tsulukidze in Kutaisi, lays special emphasis on the militant friendship and active cooperation between the Russian and Adzharian peoples.

OTHER MUSEUMS

As the days pass, your guide becomes increasingly desperate to find ways of filling up your time. Fortunately for him, museums are a growth industry in the Soviet Union, fulfilling three important functions:

- providing locales for the population to spend their leisure time in harmless, centrally-heated tedium;
- creating employment for idle *babushkas** as supervisors;
- mopping up industrial surplus.

As a result of the third condition, which *particular* museums flourish in a given town will be determined by local economic factors:

(*a*) *Politizdat* (Political publishing house) frequently over-estimates the voracity of the Soviet people's appetite for reams of obscure dialectical drivel. All unsold twenty-volume sets of their collected

* *Babushka* Grandmother, though not to be confused with the frail, silver-haired old lady who sends you a pound on your birthday (see chapter five).

works, along with a few back-issues of *Scientific Marxism*, form a good basis for the collection of the local *Museum of K. Marx and F. Engels*.

(*b*) At the close of a particularly lean tourist season, a large residue of ornamental hand-painted wooden spoons and lurid polka-dot tea sets in souvenir shop stockrooms may provide sufficient justification for setting up a *Museum of History and Local Lore*.

(*c*) A collection of army surplus shells and rocket launchers is all that is required for a *Museum of the Heroic Defence of the Obscure Place*, which celebrates a courageous rearguard action during the Great Patriotic War. The location and significance of the position heroically defended is often a mystery even to locals. To the majority of British tourists, most obscure of all comes the information that the Soviets fought on the same side as us.

It is a basic requirement of any museum to be very boring, and all of the above are to be commended for discharging this duty to the full. Normally such museums are visited only by dutiful parties of Pioneers,* so your group of foreign tourists is greeted like a busload of prodigal sons. Your appearance engenders a frenzy of activity. Swarms of guides converge on you, dates and measurements blubbing involuntarily from their lips; supervisors race to unlock and illuminate chambers believed lost to humanity. Eventually you leave the museum, weighed down by new and useless information, feeling you have brought a little happiness into other people's lives . . .

---

* *Pioneers* Youth organization similar to the scouts, only instead of knot-tying and pederasty, children learn advanced bed-making techniques and are taught what a diligent and dutiful child V. I. Lenin was.

4 · Food and drink

Russian cuisine owes its continued existence to the complete suppression of the bourgeois pseudo-science of dietetics. When one considers that the Soviet diet is based around a healthy daily intake of carbohydrates and saccharine with generous lashings of grease, washed down with neat spirits, it is only natural that nutritionalists and other dangerous free-thinkers should be prevented from disseminating their profoundly anti-Soviet views.

MEALTIMES

Technically the Russians take three meals a day; that is, there are three separate linguistic terms denoting distinct gluttonous occasions, but the Russian concepts lose much in translation when lamely rendered as breakfast, lunch and dinner. Russian meals may traditionally take place at any time of the day or night, and are capable of lasting for up to eight hours. *Zavtrak* (breakfast) may be taken at any time from rising to early afternoon; *obed* (lunch) is the name given to the excuse for further belly-worship during daylight hours; while *uzhin* (dinner) caters for any unaccounted nocturnal indulgences.

Any time not accounted for by eating is ideally taken up with the preparation of the dish. Russians are great sticklers for bureaucracy, and all true Russian recipes require at least six hours, great amounts of time being taken up doing petty, finicky and ultimately useless things. Were it not for their obligations to Lenin's Behest and the Five Year Plan, Russians would probably spend all day in gratuitous gastronomic gratification.

Nowadays the constraints of the industrial working day have forced the Soviets to adopt a more familiar meal schedule. However, this concession has not been allowed to reduce the net intake. The

39

same amount of food is eaten in three short bursts throughout the day, thus adding the risk of chronic indigestion to that of long-term disorders (cardio-vascular disease, liver failure, etc.).

Intourist carefully calculates the effect of hotel catering on the visitor:

(*a*) These thrice daily excesses suggest that, contrary to bourgeois propaganda, the Soviet Union is in fact a gastronomic cornucopia;

(*b*) Cheaper and easier to administer than a heavy sedative, the gargantuan lunches ensure the neutralizing of your seditious urges to skip the afternoon excursion and wander about a bit by yourself. With all the blood diverted from your brain to your stomach, freedom of will and thought are conveniently suppressed for the afternoon. You will be grateful to be able to slump into your coach seat and become a listless receptor to an onslaught of information about local revolutionary-democrats and bicycle factories. Better still, immediately after lunch you may stagger blindly up to your room to sleep it off and remain insensible there until it is time for you to return to the restaurant for your evening booster.

Note   The fact that the restaurant food is *tasty* and *plentiful* does not affect the statutory right of the English to complain about it on the grounds that it is *foreign*.

THE SOVIET DIET

Salads

Soviet cuisine has succeeded in defusing the nutritional potential of the salad with the following modifications:

1 fortifying the woefully lacking carbohydrate/cholesterol content by banishing green vegetables and replacing them with hard-boiled egg and potato;
2 dousing the finished product with a mixture of mayonnaise and soured cream.

With a directness enforced by the Trades Descriptions Act, this salad appears on Western supermarket shelves labelled 'Russian salad'. Restaurants in the Soviet Union treat it more whimsically, each serving it up under a lavish, eponymous name ('Beryozka', 'Potsdam', etc.). This gives the impression that the Russian salad is a much more versatile and variegated commodity than the simple stereotype we know in the West. It isn't. All you ever get is the usual random collection of anything lying within the broad parameters of animal and vegetable, diced and smothered into anonymity under a gooey dressing.

Soups

As is readily acknowledged in liberal circles throughout the world, the Westerner's penchant for chicken, tomato or pea soup is a direct corollary of the prevalent cult of the individual. In the Soviet Union, such flagrant discrimination between vegetables is not tolerated. Russian soups operate on an Equal Opportunities basis, obliged to contain *all* the ideologically sound vegetables (potatoes, cabbage, onion, beetroot).

An individual soup will take its identity from the vegetable most extensively featured. Thus we have:

Borshch (beetroot soup with cabbage, onion and potato)　The Hero Soup which sparked off the revolt aboard the battleship *Potemkin*. The traditional fare of the urban proletariat, its distinctive deep purple colouring will transfer itself readily to fingers, clothes and subsequent bowel movements.

Shchi (cabbage soup with potato, onion and beetroot)　By contrast, of peasant stock. This soup is claimed to be over 1000 years old, and would be well overdue for an Order of Lenin by now, were refreshments eligible to bear such an honour.

The Russian soup has a schizophrenic quality: its identity is precariously dependent on the availability of the requisite vegetables. The soup is the matrix in which are resolved fluctuations in the harvest and hitches in the food distribution process – it is dangerously prone to last-minute changes in ingredients:

1 the failure to deliver a consignment of beetroot turns a projected *borshch* into an actual *shchi*;
2 the unexpected appearance of a beetroot mountain forces a potential *shchi* to revert to a *borshch*.

Historical note　*Borshch* is the subject of a complex paternity suit, with Byelorussia, Lithuania and the Ukraine all contesting Russia's claim to be the Fatherland of Beetroot Soup. In fact, chefs often use borshch as the battleground for petty jingoistic wranglings, channelling their nationalistic yearnings into first-strike naming of soups. In Hero-City Kiev, the meaty, plentiful beetroot soup is called *Ukrainsky borshch*, while *Russky borshch* turns out to be thin and mean with the vegetables. Russian hegemonist chefs retaliate by labelling fulsome beetroot soup *Moskovsky*, and by fobbing off the watery slops on any of the three upstart contenders against whom they nurse a particularly vindictive private grudge.

A late challenge to the title has been made by Poland, which dates the origin of borshch back to the time of the Catholic ascendancy. Considering that large chunks of Russia, Byelorussia, Lithuania and the Ukraine used to *be* Poland, the weight of historical justification seems to back her claim.

Main course

Even the most patriotic Soviet is forced to admit that the Soviet contribution to world gastronomy is paltry. Whatever fond and senile emigrés may say about the richness and diversity of Russian cuisine, Soviet chefs can hardly claim great advances in culinary matters. In seventy years of Soviet rule, just about the only new dish they've managed to come up with is the vindictive *chicken Kiev*, booby-trapped chicken filled with butter, which spurts out all over the diner's shirt at the first poke of the knife.

In fact, the Soviets are so desperate to elbow their way into the vanguard of international cuisine that they have even tolerated the rehabilitation of that most reactionary of Tsarist dishes – *beef Stroganoff*, named after a Petersburg count and imperial adviser made short shrift of in 1917.

With customary zeal, the Soviets have solved the shortcoming by prompt annexation of surrounding national cuisines. This process of gastronomic Russification usually involves a change in the name and a rationalization of the ingredients. Thus the Uzbek delicacy *pillaf*, crisp rice served with spiced meats, by missing out a few letters and their associated vitamins, becomes the exotic sounding Russian *plov*, stodgy rice with bits of meat thrown on top. In fact, the benign patronage of the Soviet Ministry of Food has done for Eastern cuisine what the scorched earth po¹ did for Ukrainian agriculture, often using approximately the same methods, as anyone who orders the Georgian *chicken tabaka* in a Russian restaurant will discover.

Russian meals are traditionally accompanied by minuscule servings of vegetables (three pieces of diced carrot, six peas, one slice of pickled cucumber). Those critics who in the past have pointed the finger and hinted at food shortages, now sit red-faced as this custom of serving vegetables in individual portions has proved to be nothing more than an anticipation of the French culinary movement 'la nouvelle cuisine'.

Potato comes in many forms – grilled, croquette, fried, etc. – but is normally served as a diluted and runny paste so as not to discriminate against customers forced to take their food through intravenous drips.

Desserts

Ice-cream is the stock dessert in the USSR, but, as it is really quite tasty, there is no room in this slanderous anti-Soviet fabrication for mention of it.

Besides this, the Soviets manufacture many light sponges and delicate pastries that simply dissolve in your mouth. The only problem is – so do your teeth. This is because Soviet confectioners give a very high profile to sugar, glycerine and vanilla essence in their wares, to the exclusion of virtually anything else. If Russians are traditionally born with a sweet tooth, the confectionary industry single-handedly ensures that they rapidly exchange it for the equally traditional mouthful of gold ones.

To counteract their absurd craving for sickly syrup-coated gateaux, Russians adopt a policy of self-abnegation in all their other desserts. For example, the traditional Russian pancakes, *blini*, are served with *either* soured cream *or* tart fruit jam, both of which succeed in neutralizing any sweetness in the dough mixture.

After denying themselves natural methods of glucose absorption (fresh fruit), Soviets eventually crack under the strain, stuffing themselves with a shop-manufactured cake and overdosing on saccharine.

Some Russian beverages

Vodka   Vodka has long carried the standard of Russian culture abroad. As Imperial Russia grew, incorporating parts of Scandinavia, Eastern Europe and Asia, so spread vodka – and with it its peculiarly Russian by-products: sound constitution, mental stagnation and fawning sentimentality.

Today, under its influence, all the peoples of the Soviet Union are united in a fraternal unsteady embrace. The shepherds of Kirghizia and the camel-saddlers of Dushanbe have given vodka a place alongside their more traditional vices of hubble-bubble pipes and green tea. Vodka has consolidated its position as the favourite tipple of Progressive Humanity, exported – along with revolutionary ideology – to many developing countries.

Wine Soviet Armenia proclaims itself the 'Fatherland of the Grape', on the absurd pretext that – according to bourgeois mythology – Noah, the mariner and Zionist activist, on coming down from Mount Ararat after the Flood, founded the Soviet wine industry by planting the world's first vineyard.

Despite this headstart on everybody else, Soviet wines have not yet established a foothold in two important world markets:

1 *The West* Experts are rather dismissive about wines not produced under strict semi-feudal conditions. If a write-up is given at all to Soviet wines it is usually cursory – dealing only with facts essential to a full appreciation of the vintage: i.e. which Great Prince's estate the vineyard previously belonged to.

2 *The Soviet Union* Soviet wines have been showered with awards at most leading wine festivals (Bucharest, Sofia, etc.), but this adulation is not shared by the Soviet in the street. Intended as a gastronomic aid, a teasing of the palate, rather than a visa-free passage to oblivion, wine is still viewed with deep mistrust by Russians.

Champagne The Soviet Wine Trade has found, much to the irritation of purists, that its products sound more desirable if marketed under exotic Western names (e.g. cognac, port, madeira, etc.), rather than those of their less internationally celebrated places of production (Moldavia, Tadzhikstan, the Checheno-Irgush Autonomous Soviet Socialist Republic).

Especially notable in this category is Soviet champagne, whose packaging and flavour has been well imitated by its French plagiarists. This green-bottled, plastic-corked beverage comes in three varieties: dry (sweet), medium-sweet (extremely sweet) and sweet (syrup).

Prior to the Great October Socialist Revolution, the accepted way to drink champagne was with caviare sandwiches in a box at the principal opera house, watching countesses and hussars through a lorgnette. Such bourgeois clichés have been outgrown by the Soviet people, however, and are kept up today only by Party officials, out of respect for tradition.

Digression on obesity

If you thought your ordeal at the hands of Intourist catering was bad enough, spare a thought for the vulnerable groups within Soviet society – the young and the elderly. In the absence of the vigilant attentions of Help The Aged and the NSPCC, War Veterans are given four meals a day, while children in Pioneer camps must eat five.

Like most countries whose national cuisine features unhealthy combinations of ingredients, the Russians are excessive and obsessive eaters. Though, given the climatic conditions, it is hardly surprising if Soviets generally elect to put a few metres of fat between themselves and the outside world.

This is not, however, the decadent obesity which comes from gratuitous over-eating, as exhibited by middle-aged Americans who flaunt their paunches as a symbol of wealth and godliness. In the Soviet Union, corpulence has been nationalized; millions of people, from all social classes, have been enfranchised with the right to bear guts. Soviet obesity is democratic obesity – that born of nutritional ignorance and the provision of an unbalanced carbohydrate diet.*

Do not, though, expect your own trim waistline to score any ideological points. The Soviets will just presume that you are a pathetic victim of the food shortages in the West they hear about. If you are less than three stone overweight, they will constantly tell you how thin and undernourished you are. Perfect strangers will reprimand you for your act of contributory negligence in coming to such a cold climate without having rendered yourself precaution-arily obese.

You will also find yourself socially disadvantaged if your body is toned and free of extra surface layering. Success in many aspects of Soviet life (e.g. boarding of public transport, purchasing items in shops, etc.) is dependent on your being able to hold your own against fourteen-stone *babushkas* with black belts in sumo wrestling.

---

* The maxim 'You are what you eat' is especially true of the Soviet people, whose staple potato and dumpling diet ensures that they are generally pasty and dumpy.

45

Unimaginative things to do (1)

OPERA, BALLET, FOLKLORE CONCERT

Though an unashamed boor and Andrew Lloyd Webber connoisseur back home in England, in the USSR you will doubtless insist on a visit to the opera or ballet. This pretentiousness is deservedly exploited by the Intourist Service Bureau: expropriating foreign currency from you with promises of the Bolshoi, it eventually fobs you off with the Municipal Ballet Studio.

In this Sunday league of Soviet art, performances are distinguished by:

Innovative repertoire Scorning the classics on the grounds of the technical expertise required, these troupes specialize in premiering new work: dramatized cantatas commemorating the fortieth anniversary of the Victory over Hitlerite Fascism, dance fantasias inspired by the build-up of thermonuclear weaponry and the flagrant persecution of the elderly in the West, and other avant-garde art forms on relevant and stirring themes.

Grandeur The treatment of such weighty topics requires a production of fitting magnitude – and extreme length. L. I. Brezhnev's *Virgin Lands*, which won a Lenin Prize for its racy representation of the collectivization of agriculture in the Ukraine, expands from a trim seventy pages between hard covers to an epic three hours in its stage adaptation, requiring from its audience feats of resilience and fortitude to match those portrayed on stage.

Lack of inspiration The Marxist demand that art mirror life is strictly adhered to in these productions. Just as Soviet reality is hampered by small imperfections impeding its progress towards Communism, so Soviet art is dogged by minor implementation difficulties (disharmony in the chorus, lack of coordination in the

46

corps de ballet, extremely dull subject matter) which prevent a full appreciation of the profound revolutionary significance of the work.

As your attention span has been severely reduced by the inanities broadcast on Western TV, you will be amazed at the concentration exhibited by the Soviet audience, who sit through hours of opera about the construction of cement plants in the Urals without so much as a fidget. You may wrongly attribute their immobility and blank stare to boredom-induced catalepsy in its advanced stages. In fact, a Soviet audience is characterized by its respectful and attentive attitude to culture, and by its ability to suspend for the evening primary bodily functions (discrimination, sense of humour, etc.). It sits out this august occasion, husbanding its energies for the rush for synthetic-cocoa-cream éclairs at the interval.

As your guide has told you, all the people of the Fraternal Family of Nations which comprise the Soviet Union are united in their love of singing and dancing. So wherever you are in the USSR you will be encouraged to attend a performance of the local State Folksong and Dance Ensemble.

The English are rather dismissive about this art form, their only exposure being to the suspect behaviour of Morris dancing enthusiasts spinning each other around maypoles. Soviet folklore troupes, you will be relieved to hear, are more than just a cavorting collection of the socially maladjusted. Soviet national dances, whether Armenian, Moldavian or Cherkess, offer displays of virtuosity from the entire troupe. The men perform with breathtaking agility and sustained machismo (leaping around the stage on their knees, hurling daggers at one another). The women, in their turn, complement this with dances of bashful charm and tender lyricism (i.e. the boring bits).

To the Soviet authorities, there is no sight more comforting than a troupe of young people from one of the many national minorities, dressed up in absurd regional costume, channelling all their ethnic identity into a variation of the Lithuanian barrel dance.

Unimaginative things to do (2)

VALYUTNY (FOREIGN CURRENCY) BAR

Every hotel worth its salt has a foreign currency bar where guests may enjoy the luxury of a glass of Beck's in surroundings that are a recognizable pastiche of Western elegance. Those hankering after Days of Empire will take comfort in the knowledge that, due to an unusually enlightened piece of legislation by the Supreme Soviet, Soviet citizens are prohibited from entering this little oasis of privilege.

The drawback of such places is that anything that is not actually East European currency (roubles, zlotys, etc.) counts as foreign currency. Thus, there is no real distinction made between the dollar and, for example, the Sri Lankan tamil or the Vietnamese kong. All are equally valid and completely interchangeable.

The *dramatis personae* of a typical *valyutny* bar are:

The barman   He will liberally water down your cocktail, pre-empt your offer to 'have one for himself' and give you change in Nepalese karmas. Any complaints about this behaviour should be addressed to him in his subsidiary but preferred role as bouncer.

Diverse foreign nationals   Mostly Finns, who flock to these venues in squads to contest Soviet supremacy in the World Dipsomania League. You will also come across the usual representatives of Progressive and Fraternal countries (Libya, Gabon, etc.) who have as much right to use the place as you do.

Valyutchitsy (escort girls)   They hang around these places on the off-chance of picking up exotic Western diseases or State secrets which they can then pass on to their superiors.

Those not of neo-colonial bent will be able to salvage something uniquely Soviet from the experience, by ordering a *cocktail*.

The cocktail in Britain is a rigidly-defined social institution: each has its own particular meaning – the G & T is the alcoholic equivalent of the interview suit; Pernod and Black is an alternative to glue sniffing for repentant trendies, etc.

For the Soviets the cocktail has not attained this class consciousness and remains nothing more than an excuse to appear suave, by mixing in a glass the same drinks that they would otherwise mix in the stomach. Their cocktails tend to follow a consistent pattern, e.g.

Cocktail 'Cosmos'

10 ml	vodka
10 ml	cognac
20 ml	champagne
30 ml	'fruit juice'

Notes

1 Champagne is an essential ingredient – to permit an extortionate mark-up.

2 Synthetic fruit juice is added in great proportions to smooth over the strong unpalatable alcohol.

3 The strong unpalatable alcohol is added in great proportions to disguise the synthetic flavour of the fruit juice.

4 The number of incompatible ingredients (grape/grain-based alcohols, purgatives/emetics) is maximized.

5 As a token of courtesy to the customer, the cocktail is mixed out of sight behind the bar.

PART TWO

Introduction

At some stage your sheep's heart will be tugged by the desire to deviate from your itinerary, albeit for some purpose as innocuous as a shopping expedition, a meal in a restaurant or a walk in the park. Do not accede to Intourist's generous offer to arrange and supervise this activity for you, in return for nasal payment in hard currency; the environment outside your tourist bus is actually quite manageable.

THE SOVIET STREET

The main difference between Soviet and British streets is in the *advertising*. Here, peculiarly, the sole franchise to market its wares appears to have been granted to the Communist Party of the Soviet Union. Everywhere there stand huge red and white hoardings emblazoned with this Multinational's snappy catchphrases: The People and the Party are One; Long Live the Peace-Loving Leninist Foreign Policy of the Soviet Union. Like those tacky ads on Channel Four, the founder and managing director (V. I. Lenin) often appears to give his personal weight to the company's product with a few well-chosen words ('The Party is the Mind, Honour and Conscience of Our Epoch'). Sometimes they are content to feature satisfied customers: handsome muscular tin-helmeted workers demonstrating the beneficial effects of daily adherence to Marxist-Leninist ideology.

Remember, only in the British Embassy will you find yourself wholly outside the juridical authority of Soviet officialdom. Though on the streets you are free from the vigilant attentions of your guide, you have now entered the sphere of influence of the *traffic policeman*, who, despite his official calling, gets most of his job satisfaction from cautioning pedestrians. Be warned that the slightest incursion into

53

his territory (i.e. setting foot in the road) will be met with stern blasts on his whistle and the imposition of an 'on the spot' fine.

LAYOUT OF TOWN

Most cities are currently implementing a Master Plan of Reconstruction which involves the demolition of all original features and their replacement with modern sixteen-storey blocks. By the time this book is published all Soviet cities should be geographically identical and conform to the 'Plan of any Soviet City' opposite.

Urban planners have named the streets on a sliding scale of revolutionary credentials:

Principal avenues and squares are named after:
1 V. I. Lenin;
2 Principal ideologues of Marxism–Leninism (K. Marx, F. Engels, V. I. Lenin)*
3 Progressive abstract concepts (peace, victory).

Main streets commemorate:
1 Revolutionary events;
2 Revolutionary figures;
3 Revolutionary cities;
4 Revolutionary dates.

Other streets immortalize:
1 Other names of V. I. Lenin (Ulyanov, Ilyich);
2 Revolutionary professions (lathe-turner, railway worker);
3 Industrial products.

---

* It is considered flippant to imply that famous Strugglers for Peace and Socialism should have had time for such frivolous things as first names. Such luminaries are always respectfully known by initials and surname only. Note the way we mirror this practice for similar British bores: cricketers and unread gentlemen-novelists of the mid-twentieth century.

A fascinating corollary of this habit is that bourgeois writers are not accorded the honour of initials in the Soviet Union. Russians persist in referring to Thomas Eliot and Herbert Wells.

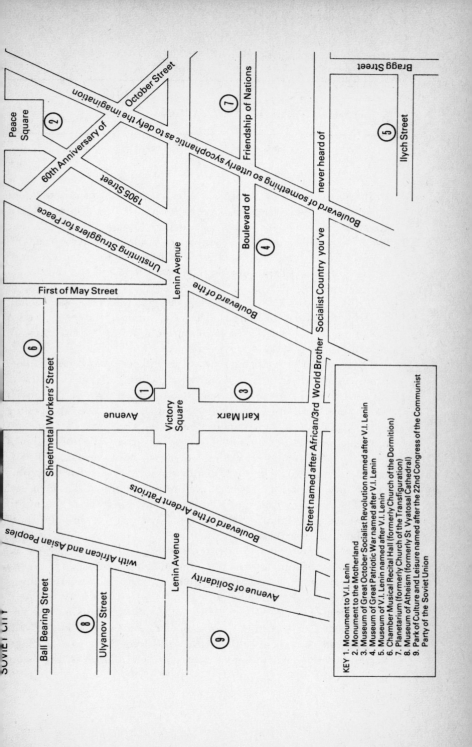

SOVIET CITY

Peace Square

② 60th Anniversary of

October Street

1905 Street

Unstinting Strugglers for Peace

⑦ Friendship of Nations

Boulevard of something so utterly sycophantic as to defy the imagination

Boulevard of something Socialist Country you've never heard of

④ Boulevard of Friendship of Nations

⑤ Ilych Street

Bragg Street

First of May Street

Lenin Avenue

Boulevard of the

⑥ Sheetmetal Workers' Street

Avenue

Victory Square

Karl Marx

① Victory Square

③ Karl Marx

Street named after African/3rd World Brother

Boulevard of the Ardent Patriots

with African and Asian Peoples

Ball Bearing Street

⑧ Ulyanov Street

Lenin Avenue

Avenue of Solidarity

⑨

KEY 1. Monument to V.I. Lenin
2. Monument to the Motherland
3. Museum of Great October Socialist Revolution named after V.I. Lenin
4. Museum of Great Patriotic War named after V.I. Lenin
5. Museum of V.I. Lenin named after V.I. Lenin
6. Chamber Musical Recital Hall (formerly Church of the Dormition)
7. Planetarium (formerly Church of the Transfiguration)
8. Museum of Atheism (formerly St. Vyatosal Cathedral)
9. Park of Culture and Leisure named after the 22nd Congress of the Communist
Party of the Soviet Union

5 · The Soviet in the street

In the West, the function of the tourist trade is to exacerbate latent racial-nationalistic tensions. Every year the British Tourist Board attracts thousands of Spanish youths to England to do summer language courses and flag the embers of xenophobia. As a trade-off, Spain annually imports coachloads of beery factory workers from Dagenham, who slob around on the Costa Brava and give a welcome fillip to anti-British feeling.

In this way British bigotry is tempered – and is fully operational, even in the *absence* of tourists. Despite having never set eyes on a Soviet, no Briton worth his salt doubts for a second that Russians are devious and unspeakable to a man, woman and child.

The Soviets share this tendency to unbridled narrow-mindedness. Left to their own devices, they would be inclined to think the worse of the British, with no provocation at all. Unfortunately, the Soviet authorities can't resist getting involved . . . and end up spoiling everything. State newspapers and television emit a constant bombardment of information about the corruption and oppression of the Capitalist system, dwelling on all its most sordid aspects – power-crazed bosses, abuse of wealth and privilege, organized crime, street violence etc. The overall picture is something like 'Dynasty' and 'The A-Team' rolled into one. Naturally, the result of this multi-media aversion therapy is that the Soviet people become quite fascinated by the West.

So, in fact, Soviets are immensely curious to meet foreigners – even if, after the intriguing abstraction presented in the press, any concrete manifestation (i.e. a live, human, awkward Brit) is bound to come as something of a disappointment.

The British tourist is a rarity in the Soviet Union. You are immediately recognizable – something to do with the cut of your clothes and the horror with which you survey your surroundings. Walking down a Soviet street, you run a gauntlet of the following polarized reactions:

(*a*) You are prey to *active pestering*.   Curious Soviets try to ascertain if you are a genuine foreigner. They sidle up to you in the street and mutter something incomprehensible – probably asking you the time, or requesting a light for their cigarette.* You blush, smile awkwardly, and shrug your shoulders. Convinced by this display of gormlessness, they scurry off to tell their families.

(*b*) You are prey to *active ignoring*.   Passing Soviets, noticing your funny accent or smelling the blood of workers on your hands, will not respond to your requests for directions to the nearest Metro. Many will shy away completely in panic, terrified of being infected by mercantilism, acquisitiveness or seditious thoughts. The more hardy, having identified an ideological enemy, will take this opportunity to vent a little Cold War aggression and barge violently past you.

After the novelty has worn off, you may begin to wish you were treated with the complete indifference which foreigners meet in Britain.

As a lone foreigner out on the streets of Russia, you are in danger of falling victim to more serious harassment:

You may be required to give informal lessons in English conversation. As you wander around the town, you may be spotted by a group of schoolchildren on excursion from Perm.† As the first foreigner they have ever seen, you present a unique opportunity to try out the English they have so laboriously committed to memory, in the language lab.

The group huddles around you, staring and whispering, and pushes forward its prize pupil – a girl in spruce school uniform complete with a lace apron, with her plaits tied by enormous red bows. Blushing awkwardly, she enunciates that collection of phonemes so often rehearsed in class: 'Speak English? What is your name? . . .'

Colossal tension reigns; the anxious teacher stands by, mouthing the words and urging the pupil on, not daring to enter the dialogue herself. The child's eyes dart nervously from the teacher to you, as she persists in her petrified interrogation.

Finally, you make some reply. There is a huge release of

---

* These questions, which in England serve as a preamble to a chat-up, are here determined by persistent economic conditions: the relative absence of functioning watches or ignitable matches.
† *Perm*   God-forsaken provincial town three days' train ride from Moscow.

suppressed hysteria – the relieved child is reabsorbed into the mass of monoglot children, the quality of Soviet foreign language instruction having been proven.

Older Soviets have a more hazy conception of the ethnographic structure of Western Europe. They seem to believe that our diversity of languages stems from the perverse dictates of our capitalist system. If we have umpteen different languages, they assume, it is in the same way that we have umpteen different brands of soap which are essentially all the same. On learning that you are English, they may well address you in German, Spanish or any other tongue of which they have a smattering.

CRITICISM

As the Soviet press never fails to point out, old age pensioners living in the concrete jungles of the dog-eat-dog West do not dare to step outside, for fear of reckless youths, rampaging and mugging their way through adolescence.

In the Soviet Union, a more humane situation operates. Rather, it is young people who walk in fear of their grandparents' generation. Indignant old folk prowl the streets, castigating and upbraiding at every step, cowing potential young hooligans into submission.

In this way, Soviet society has found a role for senior citizens, allowing them to involve themselves in public life. Unfortunately, they exhibit a disturbing tendency to involve themselves in everybody else's *private* life. At the hands of the older generation, you are likely to be subjected to the following:

Petty spurious criticism

In the West, we value very highly the individual's right to privacy. Anyone, regardless of class or race, is free to lie dying, slumped in the gutter without interference from passers-by.

Soviets, by contrast, are much more inclined to play the Good Samaritan. In fact they will not confine their attentions to those in need of succour, but will be quite prepared to stop and have a go at anyone, even if that person is quite healthy and minding his own business.*

* 'Minding one's own business' is, of course, an ideologically loaded term in the USSR, smacking of such anti-Soviet concepts as egotism and private enterprise.

This tendency to intrude stems from the fundamental belief in the perfectability of man which is at the heart of Marxist theory. Whatever it is you do, Soviets feel duty bound to come up and criticize you for it to your face.

Those social groups most at risk are:

Children After Engels exposed the nuclear family as a unit of economic oppression and servitude, Soviet society operates like an extended family. Children are not considered the private property of their parents. Everyone has a duty to help with their upbringing and promote the welfare of children, i.e. to nag parents about not wrapping their infants up warmly enough, to rap a misbehaving child over the head, etc.

Foreigners The merest deviation from the norm is heavily censured in the USSR. By the very act of being a non-Soviet in a predominantly Soviet land, you may be found guilty of stubborn individualism.

Such criticism works in inherently democratic ways. A streetful of Soviets acts like a People's Assembly: every detail of your dress or manner is avidly discussed by passers-by, and disapproved of by the majority. Your every appearance in public occasions an informal plebiscite – a Gallup poll in which passing Soviets give strident voice to their opinions of you.

Walking down the street, you will be accosted by an old woman, who asks:

Useful phrase

Молодой человек, как вам не стыдно?	Molodoi chelovek, kak vam nye stydno?	Young person, you should be ashamed of yourself.

You may be arraigned on any of the following serious charges:

- not being in possession of a hat on a cold day;
- sporting ultra-modern fashions (e.g. Adidas designer-wear);
- not managing to avoid someone walking straight into you.

Judging by the vehemence of this criticism, you may get the impression that the only things preventing the immediate flourishing of Socialist Utopia in the USSR are your hairstyle and the way you've buttoned your coat.

Note There is no particular reason why Soviets should object to your actions, except for the fact that Soviets as a collective always disapprove of anything you do as an individual, especially if it exhibits a degree of personal initiative. It is likely that, if three Soviets were stranded on a desert island, two would stand around disparaging the third's attempts to build a raft.

Ideological criticism

Sometimes you may be berated, not as an individual, but as a representative of *anti-progressive humanity*.

1 Old ladies will confront you in the street and demand to know why you want to kill their grandchildren, Sometimes they will then produce one of the urchins in question – which immediately furnishes you with several reasons.

The question is meant *figuratively*, however: viz, why is the peace-loving foreign policy of the Soviet Union matched by the aggressive adventuristic machinations of the United States and its henchmen. It is addressed to you, of course, in your informal capacity of NATO spokesman for foreign affairs.

All argument is futile, your only hope is to shed this mantle, and your dignity, to pat the brat on the head, say 'peace' with your weediest smile, and slope away.

2 War veterans will bluster up to you and subject you to a partially/totally* incoherent harangue on Second/First* World War crimes perpetrated by your country.

Note 'Your country' will be understood in the widest possible sense; you will be held vicariously responsible, at umpteen generations' remove, for atrocities committed by any Western country.

TIPS ON KEEPING A LOW PROFILE

In view of the occupational hazards of being identified as a foreigner, it is in your interests to integrate as quickly as possible into Soviet life. This process of assimilation requires a complete overhaul of your image, and the forging of a new corporate identity.

---

* According to age of interlocutor.

(*a*) First of all, you must alter your *general attitude in public*. Unlike Westerners, Soviets do not like to draw attention to themselves by frivolous exhibitionism (holding hands in public, talking, etc.) They prefer not to differ from the norm in social situations. It is unlikely, for instance, that break-dancing will ever catch on in the USSR.

The public face of the Soviet is serious and unflamboyant. Modelling themselves on the grim proletariat of the propaganda posters, they do their best to look earnest and stern – which makes them appear to newcomers as drab and morose.

This humourlessness in public is partially determined by historical factors. In the past, excessive shows of emotion on the streets have led to misunderstandings with trigger-happy Tsarist police.

(*b*) Secondly, you must make radical alterations to your *clothing*. In the West, it is fashionable to dress so as to *épater les bourgeois* – especially if you happen to be bourgeois yourself. Half of Western youth is decked out in scruffy overcoats, or else sports a nice line in neo-Fascistic leathers – all intent on provoking some kind of response from the general public. Outrageous dressers expect to evoke either *anger* or *awe*, depending on the age, shockability, etc. of the passer-by. Either reaction is equally flattering to the dresser's ego.

In the Soviet Union, by contrast, the bourgeoisie as a class has been liquidated. Its replacement as arbiter of fashion is the proletariat, which is generally a lot easier to *épater*. As a rule of thumb, the average Soviet will be about as reactionary and shockable as your grandmother. (NB: for Soviet grandmothers, add an extra six generations.)

So the Soviet Union is where Western trendies get their comeuppance. Any Western man doing something as innocuous and unoriginal as wearing an earring will be considered mentally deranged and openly laughed at.

Of course, *you* need not worry yourself about that. Fully outfitted by Marks and Spencer's, you will go down well in the USSR. Your dress-sense combines the two fashion features which Soviets respect most: 'Westernness' and total lack of inspiration.

6 · Public transport

SECTION ONE: UNDERGROUND

Most major Soviet cities now enjoy the convenience of a Metropolitan named after V. I. Lenin.*

- In Moscow, Leningrad and Kiev, the V. I. Lenin Metropolitans are styled on the Western model: rapid electric trains, running on a wide network of interconnected lines, service the whole city, bringing millions of people daily into the centre.
- Certain progressive cities (e.g. Hero-City Minsk) boast a more typically Soviet set-up: an intricate system of hoardings links dug-up and devastated major landmarks and thoroughfares. The V. I. Lenin Metropolitan exists in a Trotskyite limbo of Permanent Construction.†
- In most Asian capitals, the V. I. Lenin Metropolitan has not yet developed beyond a speculative memo in the City Planner's in-tray. The go-ahead is being held in abeyance until the second-hand purchase of the old Bombay system has been successfully completed.

Conditions

If you can overcome your vertigo and take the plunge down the

---

* To underscore its seniority, the Moscow underground is named after V. I. Lenin *twice*: officially designated as 'The Moscow Order of Lenin Metropolitan Named after V. I. Lenin'.
† It is something of a mystery why the construction of an *under*ground transport network should necessitate so much *over*ground destruction. Minsk has been largely impassable for years, as the honour of completing its Metro has been modestly deferred by successive Five-Year Plans. However, construction work is well underway, and, if all goes according to plan, the first line should be opened – along with all the shops – to mark the arrival of Communism (see page 79).

astoundingly steep escalators (an experience not unlike negotiating a ski-jump of gradient 1:2), you will enter a lost world of elegance and splendour that has been eradicated from all other aspects of Soviet life. The Metro hallways are underground palaces: vast and spacious, walled in huge slabs of white marble, with chandeliers hanging weightily from vaulted ceilings. There is an aura of gold and diamond, a hint of a former age. There is also a mob of morose Soviet commuters which completely dispels this wondrous vision.

The décor consists of:

1 regulation issue statues of heroic lathe-operators and dairy-maids;
2 any incidental plugs for Soviet society.

Thus Mayakovsky station boasts huge menacing mosaics of the poet-revolutionary's face, while at Technological Institute station, iron lettering proudly proclaims the dates of Soviet technological advances (viz. 1895 – Popov's invention of the radio, 1874 – Kolokolnikov's demonstration of the telephone).

The stations are kept spotlessly clean, controversially employing the services of *cleaners*, who prevent the laying down of a geological substratum of trampled copies of the *Standard*, Coca-Cola cans, cigarette packets, etc. Indeed Russians are fond of boasting that the floors are 'fit to eat off'. Soviet society's utopian credentials would be boosted further if it were able to advance the same assurances for its tables and crockery.

What is even more remarkable – and can surely only be explained in terms of the inherent contradictions in Marxism – is that the Underground system contrives to be *extremely efficient*. One rarely has to wait more than ninety seconds for a train. Indeed, so confident are the authorities in their ability to maintain this service that at the end of each platform there are large digital clocks which measure off the time that has elapsed since the last train departed. If more than two minutes are clocked up, one is entitled to accuse the station supervisor of revisionism.

How to find a Metro station

If you happen to be strolling along a main street, with no intention of breaking off your walk, Metro stations are generally fairly easy to come across. They are identified by a large cyrillic 'м' in blue neon, making them not unlike a certain familiar American high street institution. Indeed this resemblance may cause involuntary Pavlovian stomach spasms in the more discerning Westerner.

How to pay

Each journey costs five kopecks regardless of distance. There are no ticket collectors. Instead, the whole system is operated on a trust basis – backed up by some pretty vindictive technology.

For the law-abiding citizen, the process is simple: you place your coin in the slot by the barrier, wait for the red light to turn green and pass through.

Certain unprogressive elements try to avoid payment by walking straight through the barrier. The debilitating blow to the crotch immediately delivered by the automatic buffers has ensured that this undesirable social subgroup will be extinct within a generation.

How to find your way

Western underground systems make certain patronizing concessions to the ignorance and illiteracy of foreigners: lines are distinguished by colour, name, number, indication of direction, etc. The V. I. Lenin Metropolitan, based on a peculiar logic free of Socratic or Cartesian sullying, expects the most from the user. All aids to comprehension have been replaced by the following bewildering features:

1 In the West we combine a lack of imagination with a desire for easy orientation, and habitually name a station in honour of its place of location (Piccadilly Circus) or after a well-known monument in the vicinity (Hôtel de Ville). By contrast, the names of Soviet stations are designed to fire the commuter with revolutionary ardour rather than give too much away about the station's actual location. A nearby place will be commemorated only if no obscure Deed of the People or Socialist Realist writer springs to the mind of the Ministry of Transport official assigned the creative task of dreaming up names for stations.

2 The lines are designated only by the two termini. As these tend to be whimsically-named microregions, the average commuter would be better off with a compass and a wet finger in the air. After all, how many Londoners would know what was meant by the Hainault–West Ruislip line?

3 Western civilization has easily integrated the concept of the *interchange*, that is *one* station where *two* or more lines intersect. The Soviets strangely find this notion impossible to grasp. Consequently, a station where there is an interchange on a V.I. Lenin Metropolitan is given several different names – one for each line that meets there.*

Do not count on the luxury of a consultation with a map before you plunge into the underworld. Personal pocket maps are impossible to obtain, and the only wall map in the whole station is situated in the entrance hall. However, you are always too preoccupied with passing the clashing rocks of the ticket barrier with intact genitalia to remember this until you are half-way down the escalator.

Once you get used to the lateral-minded organization of the Soviet Metro, you will find that a change from the Gorkovsko–Zamoskvoretskaya Line to the Zhdanovsko–Krasnopresnenskaya Line at Pushkin Station/Gorky Station is really quite trivial.

Getting on

Off peak   A dignified step through the door.

Rush hour   Suicidal fling at the coagulated mass of flesh that bursts out of the doors like a paunch from American golf trousers.

Getting off

Rush hour   The usual Queensberry rules apply.

---

* Imagine the effect if this system was adopted on the London Underground. Even the English deferentially accord the seven-line interchange at King's Cross *two* names (viz King's Cross/St Pancras). The Soviets would find even this confusing and would convert it into *seven* different stations. The names of these new stations would be determined as follows:

two conceded to nearby places (provided they are fairly obscure) – *Pentonville, Clerkenwell*;

two assigned to revolutionary paraphernalia – *Hammer and Sickle, Proletariat, Red Star*;

three accorded to famous writer–agitators – *Dickens, Bragg*.

Note how this system effortlessly quadruples the number of stations on any conventional network, ensuring that the region of the brain reserved for speculative thinking is given over instead to overflow storage space for underground station interchanges.

Off peak   Though lulled into somnolence by the strangely peaceful atmosphere, do not lose count of passing stations. Remember, the interior décor of Soviet stations tends to dwell exclusively on the deeds of Heroes of the Great Patriotic War and the achievements of Leninism. Minority interest information (such as the name of the station) is given only by a small slurred voice over the intercom* – scant help to foreigners who have not yet worked out how the backwards 'R' is pronounced.

The same unobtrusive voice warns passengers of the imminent shutting of the automatic doors. As the doors follow closely the design of the automatic ticket barriers, and are not covered by the Helsinki agreement, you are advised to pass through them with extreme caution.

Behaviour

On the London Underground, regulations are relatively lax. You must refrain from smoking, putting your feet up on the seats and mugging fellow passengers but, apart from these minor restrictions, you are free – to make eye contact with other passengers, wear slightly individualistic clothing, talk above a whisper, etc.

Regulations on the Soviet Metro are rather more strict. On the wall of every carriage there is posted a code of conduct – an exhaustive list of rules governing all aspects of behaviour. Most human situations have been foreseen and expressly forbidden. A selection of rules follows:

1.2 Passengers may not use the Metro in an 'unsober condition'. If properly applied, this rule would justify the evacuation of all Metro stations for most of the day, so it tends to be waived.
1.4 Passengers must be polite to fellow passengers at all times. Through a self-imposed amendment to this subsection, old women are exempt from this obligation and are entitled to point out to you any petty detail of your behaviour or appearance that offends them.
2.3 Passengers must not lean on the escalator handrail. This regulation has been largely effective in stamping out in the USSR the crime of habitual and flagrant leaning, which threatens to reach

---

* Contrast the modesty of the Soviet station with the morbid identity crisis exhibited by Baker Street station, which displays its name six times on each square metre of wall space.

epidemic proportions in Western society. Soviet passengers now maintain an erect posture on the escalator before slumping into their seats on the train.

3.2 Passengers must space themselves evenly along the platform when waiting for trains, and must not all cluster in one place.

4.2 Reserves most seats for Invalids of the Great Patriotic War, Heroes of the Soviet Union, etc. Unless you have special clearance, it is likely that any wilful downward motion of the buttocks will constitute an infraction. If you are in any doubt as to your status, it is better to be on the safe side and stand.

In the face of this complex legislation, you may wonder what is actually permitted. Simply observe and imitate your law-abiding fellow travellers: *either* absorb yourself in a weighty tome on astrophysics *or* slump obliviously on to your neighbour.

Useful expressions

Молодой человек, как вам не стыдно?	Molodoi chelovyek, kak vam nye stydno?	Young person, you should be ashamed of yourself.

This can be used:

- to anyone breaking the written rules;
- to anyone breaking the unwritten rules (e.g. looking happy);
- to a young woman sitting with her legs uncrossed.

Personnel

The Metro stands as one of the proudest achievements of the Soviet Job Creation Scheme (Marxism–Leninism), with an average ratio of four sinecures to each useful duty. The following inventive approach to employment could serve as a useful model for recession-hit Britain:

Barrier overseer Ensures that passengers pass the fully-automated barriers in accordance with the spirit of Proletarian Internationalism. In the event of an electrical failure, she strikes recalcitrant commuters in the groin with a large knout.

First aid attendants Recover transgressors from the viciously retributive barriers.

Militsia (military police) *officer* Prevents passengers at random from entering the Metro on grounds of drunkenness and cautions sexually-crippled would-be joy-riders.

Escalator supervisor Sits in a glass box at the bottom of the escalator. Is charged with ensuring that decorum and standards of decency (as outlined in tenets for escalator use, set down by V. I. Lenin) are observed at all times.

SECTION TWO: OVERGROUND

Be careful . . . once again you have betrayed your Western conditioning. What you took for a charming ramshackle Transport Museum is in fact the Central Trolleybus Depot – a major terminus in the public transport network. There is no Transport Museum, for the simple reason that there is no means of transport so primitive that it has yet become obsolete in the Soviet Union.

Thanks to the March of Progress, however, the larger Soviet cities can now hold their own with any of the major post-Depression European capitals – enveloped in a quaint morass of criss-crossing wires, pylons and cables which line every street, blocking out the sunlight and jamming Radio Free Europe.

As twentieth-century readers may be unfamiliar with some of the vehicles still commonly used in the Soviet Union (trams, trolleybuses etc.), some simple user instructions are appended.

London commuters are used to facing the frustrations of an irregular, expensive service plagued by traffic jams. In the Soviet Union, all such problems have been eliminated. Buses do not roam around in packs, but come one by one at regular intervals; the tariff is modest; roads remain refreshingly free from traffic congestion.

How has the alleviation of traffic jams been achieved? Simply by the complete eradication of private transport since the Great October Socialist Revolution. Public transport vehicles now have a virtual monopoly of the streets.

The unfortunate corollary of this emancipation is that public transport is vastly oversubscribed. As the laws of thermodynamics do not allow congestion to be eradicated it has merely been *displaced*. All the scenes of hot, sticky, bad-tempered, impatient, impotent, claustrophobic frustration so familiar to Western commuters caught in traffic jams are still to be found in the Soviet Union, only now

68

they are *within* public transport vehicles. Congestion is safely hidden from the eyes of the people who matter – Party members and tourists, both of whom enjoy the convenience of private transportation.

This cramped environment seems to suit the Soviets, who, like woodlice, thrive on huge population density and instinctively seek out propitious conditions for prompt asphyxiation. Observers are fond of seeing in this a truly Russian characteristic – an innate sense of community, a love of togetherness. Soviets ignore all romanticizing and grimly elbow their way on.

Efficiency*

The public transport system is very regular. Wearied British commuters, accustomed to waiting half an hour for a fully-laden bus to sail indifferently past, will be glad to learn that in the Soviet Union fully-laden buses arrive every two minutes. However, the potential efficiency of the system is never realized 'for technical reasons' – usually a combination of obsolete and defective vehicles and operator incompetence.

Trolleybuses and trams are particularly irksome in this respect as they frequently become detached from their overhead power cables. This heralds an amusing silent movie routine in which the driver clambers up the ladder on the back of the vehicle and, balancing precariously on the roof, pokes around at the overhead cables with a large stick, climaxing by electrocuting himself.

Having said this, a journey by Soviet public transport should be at least a once-in-a-lifetime experience, especially for those without a first-hand acquaintanceship with the Black Hole of Calcutta.

Where to find one

Public transport stops are designated by a Cyrillic letter on a small and totally unobtrusive sign suspended over the road: 'A' for bus,

---

* There is no word in the Russian language for 'efficiency'. In an attempt to translate this profoundly alien concept, the dictionary offers 'qualified', 'skilled', 'aim-orientated' and 'working with a high coefficient of useful action'. This last, whilst undoubtedly the most accurate, is so neatly couched in Party gobbledegook as to render it incomprehensible.

The artificial word 'effektivny', considered to be both linguistically and conceptually German in origin, is associated with thrift and embryonic fascism, and is thus regarded with suspicion.

and 'T' for trolleybus or tram. Buses will approach the kerb when picking up or setting down passengers. Trams and trolleybuses are prevented by their rails/wires from making any small beneficial detours to the pavement. Passengers are therefore advised to exercise extreme caution when boarding or alighting from such vehicles, as it is necessary to negotiate a hostile lane of traffic.

How to get on

As the rickety doors shudder aside to reveal piles of suffocating bodies, panic-crazed children and old people desperately clambering towards the exit, the novice will hesitate before mounting what appears to be refugee transportation on fire. The experienced traveller, however, will not shirk the prospect of nuzzling erotically up against a sweaty stranger, but will just leap right on.

The main thing to remember is to keep your elbows cocked and at the ready. This will help you to fend off the flailing elbows and knees of other passengers, and to assure a grip round the bellies and buttocks of travellers better placed than you.

How to pay

There is a flat rate for a journey of any distance: three kopecks for trams, four for trolleybuses, five for buses.* As a remarkable gesture of the State's confidence in the honesty and maturity of its subjects, payment is left to the conscience of the citizen and is not enforced by the uniformed presence of a conductor. The procedure is as follows:

1 There is a ticket dispensing machine located on the exact diametric opposite side of the vehicle from where you happen to be wedged. The money is passed forwards along a grudging human chain until it reaches the machine. The dispensed ticket is then returned to you by the same route.

2 Those passengers foresighted enough to have purchased a book of tickets in advance enjoy no special privileges. They must in similar fashion pass one of the tickets to be punched in the *kompostor*.

The passage of coins follows the path of least resistance around the vehicle, clashing with the contraflow system of tickets being

---

* Except in Moscow, where, 'according to the wishes of the workers', all fares have been increased to five kopecks.

passed to be punched, making it difficult not to become involved in at least one of them.

The Keeper of the People's Conscience is the old woman seated to your right. Should you omit to buy a ticket, she will point out your oversight with a sharp prod. One sometimes wonders whether the prime mover behind her action is a highly-developed sense of integrity or the insatiable curiosity about the affairs of others that is given free rein in a society where privacy and individualism are discouraged.

Finding the right change in a suffocatingly overcrowded bus can also prove problematic. This cherished routine (fumbling in pockets, spilling your mandarins under the seat, dropping incriminating documents, etc.) provides much amusement for your fellow passengers. It should not be shirked by doing the preparatory searching before embarking. This is against the ethos and traditions of public transport.

Should you manage to evade the senior citizens vigilante group and 'travel like a hare',* you must keep a look out for roving ticket inspectors. Their presence is signalled by a sudden exodus of moustachioed men in Adidas hats. They may impose an on-the-spot fine of three roubles if you do not have a ticket in your possession or in transit.

Travelling posture

There are three states in which you may travel.

1 *Seated*.
Actually it is rarely possible to sit down as:
(*a*) most seats are reserved for the usual classes of undeserving citizens (e.g. Heroes of the Soviet Union, Cavaliers of the Order of Glory – Third Class);
(*b*) all other seats are reserved by obese old women and censorious old men, who enjoy exalted rank in Soviet society out of deference to their age, experience and general cantankerousness;
(*c*) Soviet vehicles are provided with fewer seats than their British

* *To travel like a hare* To joy-ride. The derivation of this homely expression is obscure, though there is almost certainly a proviso in the exhaustive regulations which expressly forbids hares and other mammals of the genus Lepus to use public transport.

71

counterparts, the standard capacity being fixed at: 16 seated, 100 standing, 251 stacked.

2 *Standing*.

There are three places you should *never* stand.

(a) By the door. You will be sorely abused, both verbally and physically, as you are battered back and forth like a shuttlecock by each wave of boarding and disembarking passengers. If a particularly large group exits at the same stop, you may be borne along with them for several hundred yards.

(b) Far away from the door. You will be unable to reach the exit in time for your stop without careful advance planning and elaborate tunnelling equipment.

(c) By the ticket dispenser. You will be pestered throughout the journey by incessant, insistent, nagging requests to tear off tickets for other passengers.

3 *Hanging off*.

BEWARE: for hardy Soviet travellers only, preferably those who have undergone para training. By all means stand back and admire this popular tradition, *but under no circumstances attempt it yourself*.

A tram crammed to the point at which passengers are being puréed within will not deter others from trying to get on. The knack is at the last possible moment before the tram departs, fling yourself at the entrance, ensuring that you become wedged in the automatic doors. As there is no 'recoil' mechanism, you will be able to travel at least as far as the next stop in relative comfort.

Note There are severe occupational hazards. Frustrated queuers, unable to get on themselves, may vent their anger on your exposed extremities. Passengers inside may vindictively demand you pay your fare, mindful of the fact that your wallet is travelling externally.

Travelling conditions

In Soviet public transport – as in the heart of a collapsed matter star – certain physical and metaphysical laws which you had believed universal are wholly negated.

For example, remove your feet from the ground and you will remain suspended, defying gravity, held firmly by the pressure from the titanic busts and buttocks that surround you. Similarly, the power of free will is accorded only to the lowest joint of your little finger.

In the cornucopia of the Soviet tram, one may observe important innovations in other fields:

Safety and comfort   No other country in the world can boast such sophisticated shock absorbing devices, in which passengers are individually cocooned in a mass of sweating human blubber.

Friendliness   As you will observe, Soviet commuters are a close-knit and indeed inseparable fraternity. The authors have heard reports that this enforced intimacy has occasionally led to anonymous sexual encounters, but have not personally been privileged to participate in any such unsavoury liaison.

How to get where you want to go

No matter where you wish to go by public transport, you will almost certainly end up somewhere else. This will, of course, provide you with a splendid opportunity to familiarize yourself with some of the more remote uncompleted 'microregions'.

If you try to implement finicky Western notions of actually ending up where you intended to go, other factors come into play:

- there is no conductor to clarify any confusion in the timetable or route;
- stern notices forbid any disturbance to the driver who is 'struggling for a Hero of Labour award';
- there is simply no point in turning to other passengers for assistance. They will not know where Proletariat Street is either, but – not wishing to appear unhelpful to an 'esteemed guest' – will nevertheless encourage you with abundant and totally fallacious directions.*

In case you should resort to independent initiative to determine where the bus is heading, public transport imposes a unique form of *total sensory deprivation*:

- your view is obstructed by a forest of fur hats and thick permafrost on the window;
- the ancient tape-recorded broadcasting of the name of the stop,

---

* No one fully understands why Soviets lie to foreigners so often. This phenomenon may have a range of motivations, from panic to a hidden manifestation of the class war.

which squeaks out of the tannoy, is incomprehensible even to native Russian speakers;

- as an afterthought, the powerful aroma of sunflower seed oil which permeates all public places in the USSR, incapacitates your nostrils.

How to get off

Buses are equipped with a small bell, positioned near the door, ostensibly for the convenience of passengers wishing to get off. In fact, an alarm chain would be more appropriate as you are generally stranded far from the exit and being trampled underfoot at the very moment you want to alight.

The bell's function is limited anyway, as nothing as innocuous as the tiny ting of a bell could induce a driver intent on finishing his run as early as possible to stop. Thus the bell is principally ornamental – it lights up an attractive sign claiming 'stop requested'.

Useful phrases

There is only one phrase you will ever hear uttered on public transport:

| Вы сейчас выходите? | Vy seechas-vykhoditye? | Are you getting off at the next stop? |

This question is the oral equivalent of Chinese water torture. It will first be put to you as you get on, then at ten second intervals during the course of your journey, until finally you are driven off by what appears to be a hostile barrage of public opinion.

In fact, one should not take offence, as the question is not asked out of rudeness or even the Soviets' deep concern with the affairs of others. It is merely that a passenger wishing to make a sortie must first establish whether he has enough cohorts to mount a feasible putsch.

Thus the question serves as a prelude to: *either* (if your answer is 'no') barging past you and elbowing you in the ribs; *or* (if the answer is 'yes') tagging on to your clothing and breathing halitosis down your neck.

It is uncommon to indulge in idle conversation on buses, as oxygen must be conserved, so most communication is conducted well below the verbal level:

- Ticket thrust up your nose = 'Could you punch this please?'
- Rabbit punch to kidneys   = 'Are you getting off at next stop?'
- Straight-arm lift by throat = 'This seat is reserved for . . .'

Things to do (1)

ROCK CONCERT

A rock concert is a rare event in the USSR, and all gigs play to packed Palaces of Culture. The audience is well-behaved by English standards, sitting tidily and clapping at the end of each number. The tone is set by the many frowsty colonels and Heroes of Labour, allocated the best seats to all cultural events, who survey the concert with the same polite boredom they experienced at the Plenary sessions of the 27th Party Congress.

On the Soviet rock circuit, you can catch the following:

1 Soviet home-grown talent: internationally-acclaimed bands (Stas Namin Group, the Happy Boys), as well as lesser-known rock ensembles from Chelyabinsk.
2 The cream of young Western talent: Cliff Richard, John Denver, the Dooleys.
3 Western artistes in exile.

While much media coverage is given to Nureyev, Baryshnikov and other Soviet defectors, it is not generally appreciated that the USSR frequently gives asylum to Western performers denied freedom of artistic expression at home. Both *Greg Bonham* and *Dean Reid*, barred from performing in their native lands for having dared to push back the frontiers of mediocrity, now enjoy superstar status in the Soviet Union . . . for the minor concession of having their royalty cheques made out in roubles.

Among Soviet groups, the favourite genre is *hard rock*.* However,

---

* Although the rest of Europe had been living by it since 1582, Russia – for reasons of religious stubbornness – did not adopt the Gregorian calendar until 1917. As a consequence, the Soviet Union is currently living in 1973 and musical taste is accordingly dire.

76

the idea of any one band cornering a particular style or image and claiming it as their own has an anti-Soviet smack of monopoly and elitism. The Soviet gig is, rather, more of a circus, in which the musicians try to impress with their versatility. The set usually includes a close-harmony folk song, a rockabilly number, extracts from the classics, and possibly some yodelling or tap-dancing as an encore.

All this is performed with the smell of freshly-ignited thunder-flashes and glint of gold lamé, stirring a disturbing Proustian memory in contemporary British spectators. The musicians will be distinguished in two ways:

1 *Extreme age* This is not because they have been on the road for twenty years, but because Soviet hard rock is a carbon copy of its English model. Checking out their Deep Purple album covers, Soviets assume that this genre can be executed only by people of advanced years. They do not realize that we only allow old has-beens to stagger on to a stage and supplement their pensions out of *fondness* – because we used to like them back in the sixties when we were too young to know any better.

2 *Sartorial elegance* Again, a bit of a time warp. To demonstrate his artistry under conditions of extreme adversity, the Soviet musician manages to perform this nasty music while struggling manfully to control a rampant pair of flares.

Rock Opera

By far the most loathsome spin-off of the rock genre is the Soviet 'rock opera' – a ghastly cocktail of late-sixties riffs, expansive beards and waistlines, and mythological lyrics. It is one of the most frightening results of the liberalizing trend in Soviet society, and alone constitutes ample proof of the necessity of a speedy return to Stalinist values.

It is, of course, possible that this horrible imitation of the worst of Western dross is merely an elaborate ploy by the Soviet Ministry of Culture, designed to wean Soviet youth from this malign influence.*

* Last year saw evidence that the Soviets are beginning to outgrow their Led Zeppelin fetishism – ironically, just as English second-hand record shops began to shift their Woodstock six-album boxed sets again.

Unofficial bands

The gaff was rather blown on the Soviet *underground music scene* when its chief representative 'Time Machine' transpired to have modelled themselves on Smokey.

Though a *punk* movement exists in Leningrad, the fact that it is an arrestable offence to have green hair rather dampens its potential as a tourist attraction.

7 · Shopping

PART ONE: SHOPPING (THEORY)

Shops in the USSR are currently in a period of revolutionary transition. According to the theory, after dwelling in the propitious conditions of *Developed Socialism* for several generations, the Soviet people will be so spiritually elevated that selfishness and greed will have been totally eliminated. They will then be fit to call themselves a *Communist* society. When Communism is declared (date to be announced: see press for details), money will be abolished, all the shops will be opened, and citizens will walk in and help themselves only to what they need.

To prepare the proletariat for this great day, and to compensate for the lack of other distractions, the Soviet authorities have championed shopping as the principal national hobby.

Under Socialism, however, much of the excitement of this activity has been lost. As all shops are owned by the State, goods and prices are standardized; so bargain-hunting, which excites such fervour among shoppers in other countries, is in the Soviet Union a totally pointless activity.

To reintroduce the element of fun and challenge into shopping, the authorities have resorted to other methods:

1 Desirable items appear on the market only sporadically.
2 When they do appear, they crop up in totally inappropriate shops (e.g. a batch of umbrellas gets sold off, first come first served, in a shoe shop).

So the nation spends much of its leisure time scouring shops for elusive items, and clawing its way towards available ones.

Shopping gives the People a chance to get out for a bit of exercise: a mild warm-up (daily constitutional down the city's high streets), followed by a healthy bit of Socialist Competition (jostling and bustling for a restricted supply of goods).

Queuing

Of all the diverse tasks which constitute the constructive activity of shopping, *queuing* is without doubt the most exciting and time-consuming. The queue represents the finest achievement of the Russian proletariat – rather as football violence is the boast of the British. Responding to the call of Leninism, the Soviet people strive to make the queue the most impressive product of emergent Communism, by ensuring that their queues are *longer* and *slower* than anywhere else in the world.

The Soviet queue is not orderly and polite like its lackadaisical British equivalent. The Soviets view queuing as a full-blooded sport, requiring a lot of fancy elbow work and strong arm tactics. They eagerly take up any opportunity to engage in it – automatically joining any queue they spot.

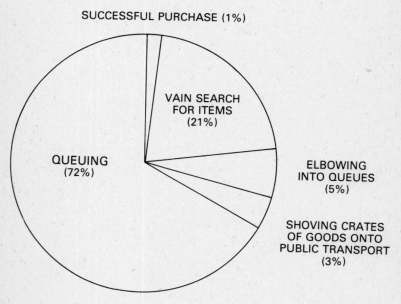

Fig. 1
Distribution of tasks in activity of *shopping*

A queue has a distinct sense of community; it works together, defending its collective interests. Any attempt to queue-barge into the front is met by a sally from the rear; and, with a tightening of the ranks and a unified push, the infiltrator is ejected.

Only Heroes of the Soviet Union are excused from queueing, and – impervious to the grumbling of other members of the queue – will march right to the front of the line. Remember that forty years ago this honoured citizen was probably riding high on the tanks of the liberating Red Army, plunging deep into the heart of Hitlerite Germany; he will certainly not let a few mild rebukes from his compatriots halt his advance now.

So that queuing should exercise the mind as well as the body, the Soviets have invented an utterly bewildering system – which could serve as an enrolment test for Mensa.

To obtain a given item, you must queue three times:

1 at the counter, to survey available goods and make a choice;
2 at the cash-desk, to pay for the item and be given a receipt;
3 at the counter again, to exchange the receipt for the desired item.

There are certain advantages to this three-tier queuing system:

(*a*) it requires three times as many staff, who, exponentially, are nine times as cantankerous;
(*b*) it requires three times as much counter space, thus reducing the amount of space available for customers;
(*c*) it takes three times as long to buy anything, thus keeping citizens out of mischief.

However, when standard methods of *queuing theory verification* are applied to this system, the following complications are revealed:

Paradigm 1.1 As none of the processes can be run concurrently, a time lag is inevitable: by the time process **2** has been completed, the item chosen in process **1** may no longer be available for process **3**.

Paradigm 2.1.1
    where X_1 = shop assistant behind counter
            Y_1 = cashier
Any process – **1**, **2** or **3** – may abort, should X_1 or Y_1 arbitrarily absent themselves.

Paradigm 2.1.2
    where X_2 = another shop assistant coming on afternoon shift
Should X_1 be replaced by X_2 in the interim between **1** and **3**, it is possible that she will refuse to enter into any transactions initiated by her predecessor.

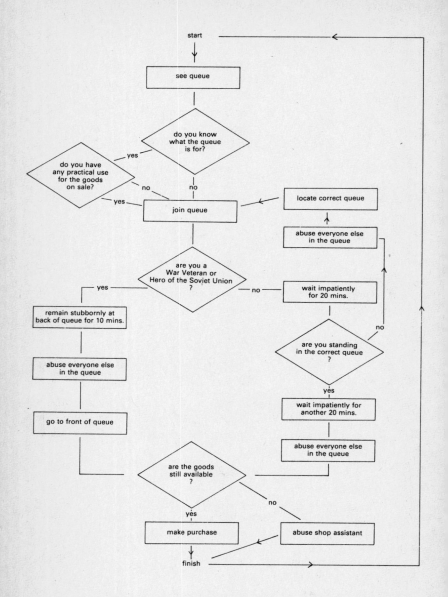

Fig. 2: Systematic guide to *shopping* in the USSR

Customer relations

As all shops in the Soviet Union are owned by the State, and no longer forced to compete with each other, there has been an end to the petty high street rivalries and wasteful 'price wars' prevalent in Western society. All the latent aggression of the shop assistant can now be properly harnessed and vented directly on the customer.

Customer/shopkeeper relations are brusque at the best of times, as the latter frequently interprets the former's attempts to purchase goods on display as an act of gratuitous provocation. Superficial pleasantries are avoided, not so much because they are superficial as because they are pleasant.

The notion that 'the customer is always right' is resisted by shop assistants, who would be unhappy if only the *customer*'s pig-headedness were officially tolerated. They prefer to see their shop as a modern-day Forum, where customer and shop assistant can engage in free and frank discussion – ranging from the availability of consumer goods to comments on one another's age and racial origin.

These arguments often arise as a result of small misunderstandings, prompted by the following:

1 the special storage surcharge levied on certain deficit items, payable directly to the shop assistant;
2 the 'No Smoking' rule which applies in all public buildings – not so much for health reasons as for disciplinary purposes.

However, such confrontations are usually short-lived, as there is an army of surplus staff on hand to strengthen the official position. The shopper is unlikely to get much support from the other members of the queue, as Soviets instinctively side with authority over the individual.

Customer services

All technological innovations are given a minimum fifty-year trial period in the West before being introduced into Soviet society. For this reason, the *cash register* is only just beginning to gain widespread acceptance in shops over the preferred and far less incriminating *abacus*.

The concept of *credit*, which propagates the Capitalist myth of trust, is still totally shunned, though Soviet economists have noted with interest the impressive stagnatory effect that the use of a single Barclaycard can have on the forward motion of a queue.

Superficial pleasantries are avoided . . .

Pending the introduction of the *plastic bag* (*c.* 1990), which is still undergoing stringent tests for dangerous side effects, Soviets shop with the use of an *avoska* (string bag).

NB Some kind of carrier bag is essential, as all goods, once purchased, are wrapped up into *large brown-paper cones* − a shape which makes it impossible to carry *three* such items without dropping at least *one* of them in the mud.

Shopping hours

1 Besides operating lunch hours which may occur at any time between elevenses and teatime, many shops also close in the afternoon for a mysteriously-named 'sanitary hour'.
2 Stock-taking is a major source of irritation to the shopper as, for bureaucratic reasons, all chemists close on one day and all stationers on another − rendering it impossible to attempt to buy the goods which they probably don't have anyway.
3 In common with just about everything else in the Soviet Union, shops are quite capable of being closed 'for technical reasons'. This is especially puzzling in view of the total absence of technology.

Useful phrase

У нас не бывает   Oo nas nye buivayet   We don't have it.

This is employed by shop assistants in response to a routine enquiry about the availability of any consumer goods.

Note   Philologists will be intrigued by the strange use of the Russian imperfective tense, implying that the item is not stocked, has never been stocked, and will never be stocked.

SECTION TWO: SHOPPING (PRACTICE)

From the outside, Soviet shops are plain and unpretentious. The Western shopper, accustomed to being courted by glossy advertising and slick window-dressing, may even find them drab. The squat lettering on the shop front does not denote the proprietor or brand-name, but rather indicates the product theoretically stocked within, e.g. *Ovoshchi* (vegetables), *Frukty* (fruit), *Golovny ubor* (head-dresses).

The inside of a Soviet shop, by contrast, is a hive of activity. Queues form and disband, merge and coagulate – like oil slicks in those absurd lamps you find in dentists' surgeries. The Soviet shopper throws herself around like a jobber on the Stock Exchange: pushing in here, reserving a place there, spotting an embryonic queue at 200 yards. As consumers rush from one queue to another in Brownian motion, a joyful chaos reigns – customers collide, paper cones rip open, newly-purchased mandarins are trampled beneath the feet of a thousand stampeding shoppers . . .

Knigi (Bookshops)

A nineteenth-century anarchist with a beard once remarked: 'All the works of Pushkin are not worth one well-made pair of boots.' To discourage thinking in such futile materialistic terms, the Soviet authorities have now made both the contested items unavailable. Instead of outmoded classical texts (Dostoevsky, Tolstoy) and minority-interest literature (poetry, humour), bookshops specialize in:

Scientific Rejecting bourgeois mysticism (sociology, psychology, genetics, etc.), Soviet academicians have pioneered their own bodies of ideas: Scientific Communism, Scientific Atheism, and other innovative modes of thought – which they propound in vast and incomprehensible volumes.

Soviets also have a love for aeronautics, cybernetics and hydraulic engineering, especially if they are presented in dry factual form, with lots of bar charts and statistical tables.*

Socialist Realist literature Unlike their Western counterparts, Soviet authors are not forced to pander to the tastes of a fickle populace in order to live by their writing. They need pander only to the more predictable tastes of the *State Publishing House* (*Gosizdat*).

This body has taken upon itself the arduous responsibility of dictating the literary tastes of the nation. It feels that, after a hard day's toiling and struggling for the emancipation of all oppressed nations, the proletariat does not want to be subjected to vicious indictments of the Soviet system. Rather, it wants to put its feet up

---

* It is a common boast in the USSR that the Soviets are the best-read nation in the world. If print runs of tedious scientific pamphlets are anything to go by, then this claim seems incontestable.

and read uplifting narratives – about the proletariat toiling and struggling for everyone else's emancipation.

The few morbid intellectuals who insist on committing their own insecurities to paper are not rewarded with publishing contracts.

The Soviet reader is not deprived of foreign literature of the Socialist Realist school. Among others, *Gosizdat* publishes the work of *James Aldridge*, the literary colossus of Australia, and our own *Melvyn Bragg*, billed as 'one of the most popular prose writers of his generation'.

Political   A must for those with a keen interest in the Leading Role played by the Communist Party in all fields of human achievement.

If the Collected Speeches of the current Party General Secretary are not yet available in handsome scarlet-bound edition (a heavily-subsidized snip at 85 kopecks), of most interest to the foreigner will be volumes stocked under the category *International Relations*. These are invaluable additions to the libraries of those who wish to learn the barbaric and genocidal truth about Zionism, American imperialist expansionism and British neo-colonialism in Wales.

Often these books are available in Western European languages, specifically for those bourgeois nationals who arrogantly believe that having lived in a country the whole of their lives gives them some right to pass judgement on it. Soviet political journalists realize that, from their superior vantage point at their desks in the Ministry of Enlightenment, they are far better placed to slag off a country they have never visited.

Posters   Officially intended to step up agitation campaigns in the home, posters are in fact bought almost exclusively by Westerners as joke presents for friends back home. They are huge, gaudy and dirt cheap, and deal with the following themes:

(a) *ideological*
- artist's impression of K. Marx, F. Engels, V. I. Lenin, and M. S. Gorbachev, suitable for parading spontaneously around town on public holidays;
- portraits of V. I. Lenin in various historical poses:
  – addressing workers and soldiers from the armoured train;
  – sitting at his desk editing Bolshevik broadsheets;
  – as a baby, dressed in a sailor suit.
- the decisions of the 27th Party Congress, the Testament of V. I. Lenin, and other such information which the conscientious

citizen would wish displayed in three-foot-high letters on his bedroom wall.

(b) *political* These posters arbitrate on issues of international dispute, where Progressive Nations are struggling for their legitimate right to self-determination. To enable the observer to come to a considered and balanced judgement:
- those *fighting to throw off the yoke of imperialism* are represented as square-jawed proletarian clones with appropriate skin pigmentation – depending on whether they are liberating Laos, Angola or Palestine.
- the *forces of oppression* are portrayed as rapacious salivating skeletons emblazoned with stars and stripes and swastikas, egged on by portly capitalists with top hats, gold watch chains and dollar signs in their eyes.

(c) *economic*
- graphs showing the increases in productivity in the Soviet turbine industry since 1942;
- for more serious students: charts showing the relative economic might of East and West in *real* terms (i.e. in quantity of production of the works of K. Marx and V. I. Lenin).

(d) *social* A set of posters illustrating various aspects of Soviet life (housing, schools, clinics) contrasting them with their Western equivalent: the one being bright and colourful, the other grey and dreary. Before praising this particular artist's refreshing and outspoken honesty, note that the drab oppressive one is intended to be the *West*.

Also available are: handy pocket-sized 'photoportraits' of all your favourite Politburo members – with hairlines touched up, and birthmarks and life-support machines painted out.

Map department A chance to brush up on the relief geography of various Last Bastions of Freedom holding out against imperialist expansionism, and other countries in the Vanguard of the Socialist World (Mozambique, Kampuchea).

The only bourgeois countries included are those which are so geographically nondescript as to preclude any interest whatsoever (i.e. Netherlands).

Non-sensitive areas of the Soviet Union are copiously available. With the recent exposure of the Peters Projection as a bourgeois

88

falsification, the northern regions of Siberia are presented in their full distended glory.

Gramplastinki (Record shops)

Soviet record shops are divided into three departments.

1 *Classical music* Soviets are aware that classical music can be appreciated properly only in an atmosphere of extreme humourlessness, so the same air of austerity prevails here as in classical record departments in the West. A timid smattering of the intelligentsia creeps around in silence, sternly surveyed by an elderly shop assistant. Everyone is too frightened to buy any records.

Soviet classical recordings are highly regarded by connoisseurs. This is because the State Record Company 'Melodiya' has noticed, unlike its Western counterparts, that all classical musicians are extremely ugly, and should under no circumstances be featured on their LP covers. Soviet pressings, therefore, are issued under plain wraps.

2 *Popular music* This department is more recognizably Soviet, as swarms of warring factions descend upon the sales counter.

A wide selection of popular recordings is available, enabling one to assess the impact of Soviet culture on pop music as we know it today:

- the seminal groundwork done by the legendary Armenian and Moldavian vocal-instrumental ensembles, which led to the evolution of 'swing' in the late sixties;
- the dominance in the public's affection of *Yuri Antonov* and *Stas Namin* throughout the seventies and eighties;
- the innovative 'hard rock' sound which will be forever linked with the names of '*The Red Poppies*' and '*The Flowers*'.

Generous concessions are made to the English and American influences on the development of popular music, by including in the catalogue of artistes internationally famous mega-stars (*Dean Reid, Greg Bonham*) and progressive Western groups (*Abba, The New Seekers*).

3 *Marxism–Leninism* This is the section which is unpopulated by customers or staff. It remains, however, by far the most interesting of the three, where one may pick up, at heavily subsidized prices, the following gems:

(a) Anthems of the fifteen Soviet Socialist Republics. A stirring martial arrangement of the traditional hymns. The words, by enlightened national poets, proudly proclaim the Republic's long history of glorious servility to Russian hegemony. Flip over for instrumental remix.

(b) Collected speeches of V. I. Lenin. A must for all those suffering from speech impediments. Savour again how V. I. Lenin managed to found the First Socialist State in the World without being able to pronounce the letter 'R'.

(c) Song cycle on patriotic themes, with lyrics by poet-veteran S. P. Benke, including: 'Motherland Russia', 'Song about the Working Class', 'Lenin and the Party in the People's Heart', and others – all set to a traditional Russian melody.*

Odyezhdi (Clothes shops)

The Soviet Government is confident that its Heroic People can overcome any obstacle on the road to Communism. However, in asking them to dress tastefully while making available only the tawdry materials outlined below, it may just have overreached itself.

Colour   In the past the Russians have had something of a reputation for being drab and colourless dressers. In an effort to show what a bunch of hip daddy-os the Fraternal Soviet Peoples really are, the State Fashion House now exclusively churns out paisleys and polka-dots in shades of garish orange and purple which would have appeared outré at the Woodstock Festival.

Cut   Though fickle Western fashion cyclically turns its back on them, bell-bottoms and shirts with hang-glider collars are permanently in season in the Soviet Union. This love of surplus fabric on garments may be attributed to two factors:

1 Adherence to the theory that 'big is beautiful'. In common with the Americans, this maxim is applied principally to buildings and nuclear arsenals, but in the USSR it has spilled over into the sartorial field. It holds especially for *hats*: among hipsters (speculators, rock musicians, etc.), the bigger your fur hat, the cooler you are.

2 The Soviets are aware that all human desires are conditioned by

* To be released in England under the title 'Variations on a theme of Sycophancy'.

objective material laws. Thus, the Westerner's preference for straight trousers over the last ten years or so is clearly indicative of crises in the Capitalist economy: failure of cotton harvests, under achievement of production targets in the textile industry, etc. Anxious that the Soviet people should suffer no such privations below knee-level, the authorities ensure that enough fabric for *four* pairs of trousers is lavished on each *one*.

As a disincentive to the exercising of discrimination or dress sense, clothes are often supplied in gift packs, sold in the 'Presents for Men' section of department stores. Typically, one of these comprises: hideously mismatched lime-green shirt, orange floral tie and bottle of 'Natasha' aftershave. Devoid of taste and the spirit of revolutionary defiance, Soviet men obediently wear all three.

Unless you firmly believe that this summer really *will* be the Summer of Love again, the only Soviet clothes you may care to invest in will be:

Thermal underwear   Westerners are apt to arrive in the Soviet Union already modelling 1953 Sherpa Tensing chic. Should you forget this important survival resource, Soviet shops do a very nice line in long-johns with reinforced crotch in a rather kinky latex finish.

Beware of overdoing it on the thermals. To compensate for the arctic conditions outside, Soviet flats and public buildings are usually heated to hothouse temperatures. Should you be overinsulated, within ten minutes of entering any public building, you will experience an unpleasant and embarrassing meltdown in the uro-genital area.

Military uniform   The trendier members of your group may like to visit the *Voentorg* (military outfitters) shop. Soviet fatigue jackets are rather natty, with their hammer-and-sickle emblazoned brass buttons, and the successful purchase of an officer's uniform will be an undoubted credibility coup.

Technically, only Soviet conscripts may buy uniforms, but sometimes the sales assistant has a temporary attack of amnesia over the fact that the Soviet Army currently has no foreign legion recruited from Western tourists with strange haircuts, and sells you them anyway.

Remember: the paramilitary look has not really caught on in the Soviet Union, except among soldiers. Your perfectly vacuous reasons for wanting to deport Soviet military gear may be seen in a sinister counter-revolutionary light by customs officers.

Universam (Supermarket)

With its one-stage queuing system and simplified access to goods, the supermarket was regarded as suspiciously straightforward when first introduced into Soviet society. Certain confused individuals, doubtless mistaking this new and unfamiliar system for Communism, proceeded to take items from shelves and – omitting the tedious ritual of settling up with the cashier – made straight for the exit. To curb this premature embracing of Communism, customers are now required to leave all bags at the entrance.

Enterprising management has succeeded in impairing any potential efficiency in this new system, employing the following methods:

1 Outstandingly laborious arithmetic calculations by the cashier, hampered by Stone Age technology, ensure that the queue at checkout never proceeds at anything above action replay pace.
2 Lest staffing fall to a reasonable level, a wizened old woman is employed to sit behind the cashier and tear customers' receipts – living proof that even labour which serves no conceivable end 'ennobles man'.

The *tinning process* is still undergoing some teething troubles in the USSR, and as a result many storage products are pickled in glass jars.* Though the principle behind it was mastered by Archimedes, the screw-top still baffles Soviet technology, so the lids of jars must be painstakingly levered off with a spoon.† The only exception is *fish*, as the Ministry of Food has noticed what fun Western consumers can have trying to open the tins with the brittle and inadequate keys provided.
Fruit   In refreshing contrast to Western dieticians' idolatry of the stuff, fruit has been traditionally ignored by Russian cuisine and the Soviet Department of Trade alike. Fresh fruit is mistrusted and usually bottled on sight, though mandarins are occasionally displayed by shops as curios. Whether through disinformation or plain ignorance, fruit has become surrounded by myths and superstitions in the USSR, and apples are popularly believed to make you fat.

---

* Not least among these, of course, is V. I. Lenin, pickled for posterity in his mausoleum, where thousands of reverential tourists queue daily to visit this shrine to Soviet marination technology.
† The fact that many Russians are either *extremely obese* (women) or *inveterate drunkards* (men) may be directly attributable to the fact that neither jars nor bottles may be resealed once opened.

Vegetables   Like all other consumer goods in a Socialist economy, vegetables are marketed in one basic model. Using similar specifications to those applied to car design and architecture, the Soviet prototype vegetable is lumpen and squat (viz. potato, onion, beetroot). Foppish vegetables like broccoli and asparagus, whose delicate elegant shape and texture blatantly flaunt their aristocratic affiliations, have been widely discredited and are not generally stocked.

Do not rush into an orgy of bulk-buying when you notice jars of *ikra* (caviare) retailing for a modest few kopecks in supermarkets. Russian items of international culinary standing are invariably bastardized (compare the fate of beef Stroganoff). *Ikra* also translates as 'vegetable paste'. Instead of Beluga, you are buying aubergine mangled through a liquidizer.

Dairy produce   Due to problems in Tsarist refrigeration technology, milk is traditionally served at various stages of turning: slightly curdled (kefir), highly curdled (smetana) and completely curdled (cheese).

Confectionery   Sweets in the Soviet Union really live up to their name, being in effect little more than chocolate-covered sugar lumps. By far the most viciously saccharine sweet is the *Burevestnik*.* With Soviet dentistry still operating in a primitive state, free from Hippocratic interference, the consumption of a pack of these requires great courage – or even greater ignorance.

Beryozka (Foreign currency shops)

Shopping in the Soviet Union for the foreigner is a two-stage experience:

1 Firstly you are crushed, abused and beaten to the ground as, out of ignorance or a misplaced gesture of internationalism, you attempt to make your purchases in a Soviet shop.
2 Eventually you wise up/sell out – and enter the courteous, civilized world of the *Beryozka*.

There is an eerie ethereal air about the place: the floors are carpeted, soft balalaika music chimes in from invisible speakers,

* *Burevestnik*   Named after Gorky's revolutionary seagull. So called due to its role as Nemesis of your waistline and premolars.

goods outnumber customers, vast banks of hideous *matryoshka* dolls stare squatly at you . . .

Besides the interior décor, the *Beryozka* has certain advantages over other Soviet shops:

(*a*) *Nice things to buy*   The *Beryozka* is the repository of all deficit (i.e. luxury) items, e.g. caviare, chocolate, classical literature, politeness, hygiene, etc.

(*b*) *No Soviets*   Soviet citizens, for their own well-being, are not permitted to enter such establishments. Sometimes a policeman is stationed at the door, to prevent them from straying inadvertently in upon this ideologically traumatic vision of bourgeois self-indulgence.

Despite its seeming Westernness, the *Beryozka* has not entirely thrown off its Soviet shackles. You are warned that at least ninety per cent of the goods stocked are *totally useless* and should under no circumstances be bought.

Especially to be avoided are:

The balalaika   Triangular-shaped instrument with three strings, two of which are tuned to the same note. Potential purchasers are warned that it is not possible for this instrument to sound nice in groups of less than 100. It is also a *cliché*, and will earn you the same mockery at Heathrow customs as arriving with a ten-gallon hat from the USA or a plaster cast from Switzerland.

'Matryoshka' dolls   Tourists are strangely fascinated by the fact that these hand-painted monstrosities all go inside one another, and generally fail to realize that, besides blighting your mantelpiece for life, this is *all* they do.

Caviare   Russians find it endlessly amusing that Westerners politely refuse to admit even to themselves that the stuff is disgusting.

Busts of V. I. Lenin   Even posthumously V. I. Lenin is thought capable of generating considerable income in foreign currency, so plastic statuettes of him are reverently mass-produced. In fact, their only utility is as alternative garden gnomes.

Nevertheless the *Beryozka* is an important survival resources centre for those undergoing prolonged stays in the Soviet Union. It is not thought likely that *this* shop will be opened to the people when Communism is announced.

Things to do (2): Sports

SPECTATOR SPORTS

Sport, as an expression of the spirit of *Socialist Competition*,* is highly vaunted in the USSR. The national summer game is *football*, whilst throughout the cold winter months the Russian's bloodlust is kept on the boil with *ice-hockey*.

Football

Sponsorship in football has reached a more advanced level than in England, with whole teams being named after ideologically credible industrial or military hardware (viz. Dynamo Kiev, Torpedo Moscow, etc.).

The game itself makes rather a dull spectacle from the English point of view – for two reasons:

1 The away team has usually just flown in from outer Siberia, and has to play the whole match suffering from severe jet-lag.
2 Due to the great distances involved, there is no tradition of supporters following their teams to away matches – so hostilities are restricted to the field of play.

Ice-hockey

The intricacies of the play are fairly hard to follow, but this should not impede the spectator's enjoyment of the 'off the puck' incidents,

---

* Sometimes, by contrast, sporting fixtures are deemed a fit occasion to make a *gesture of solidarity* with Brother Socialist countries. For example, the 1982 World Cup qualifying match between the *USSR* and *Czechoslovakia*. A win for the USSR would have allowed Wales to qualify at the expense of the Czechs, so both teams observed a strict policy of non-interference in the internal affairs of the other – and neither entered the other's half of the field.

which are the game's main attraction. Indeed, the function of the sport is largely ceremonial – a show of might, rather like the Revolution Day parade of weaponry, which hints menacingly at the amount of damage Soviets can do to the opposition in the field of conventional warfare.

WINTER SPORTS

You can enjoy the whole range of winter sports at the Central Park of Culture and Leisure, which extends over the former estate (grounds, ornamental lakes, etc.) of a dynasty of nobles dispossessed by the Revolution.*

Bellicose tourists intent on waging the Cold War in every walk of life are warned to stay off winter sports, as all Soviets – even old fat ones – are very good at them. It is one thing when the plucky Brit finishes seventeenth behind packs of steroid-enhanced Slavs in the Olympic Games; quite another when you are cut up on the ice by a flabby Soviet senior citizen. Unfortunately, skills acquired on artificial ice-rinks and at exclusive Swiss ski-resorts are of little help when you skate and ski under Soviet conditions.

Skating

The Soviets have realized that, once you have mastered the art of skating without the use of the nose as a third support, the whole process becomes very tedious, there being nothing left to do but go round and round the circuit. You will find the sport more challenging on a Soviet rink which incorporates natural hazards (rocks, crevasses, etc.).

However, it is unlikely that you will get up enough speed to be inconvenienced by these obstacles, as Soviet hire-skates are made without the cosseting addition of ankle supports. This ensures that you skate like a new-born calf with a severe case of rickets. What's more, your laborious progress across the ice is not helped by being constantly buzzed by Soviet skaters, all of whom clearly harbour a secret yearning to be taxi drivers.

* The most famous is Moscow's Central Park of Leisure and Culture named after A. M. Gorky (Gorky Park). Gorky, author and revolutionary sybarite, gained a particular insight into leisure during his years of slobbing around on the Isle of Capri.

In general, you are not advised to attempt this sport unless you are already extremely proficient at it. The bourgeoisie gets a bad enough press out there as it is.

Skiing

The Soviets practise *cross-country skiing*. This variant rejects the bourgeois convention which allows us to go *down* the hill on skis and *up* the hill on ski-lifts, pedantically maintaining that if one goes *down* the hill on skis, one should go *up* the hill on skis as well. This ensures complete humiliation for the beginner, as even the most maladroit of us can contrive to look dignified in a chair-lift.

Novices may take comfort from the fact that even accomplished Alpine skiers fall over on attempting to ski cross-country for the first time. This is because the skis are attached only at the toe. This way, the Soviets claim, it is less easy to break your ankle. They gloss over the fact that this way it is much easier to part company entirely with the ski half-way down the slope and break all other parts of the anatomy.

Sledging

Snow as a commodity suffers badly from overexposure in the USSR. From an early age Soviets become quite blasé about it. Consequently, though skating and skiing, with all their Olympic credibility, are popular, sledging – a celebration of snow for its own sake – is engaged in only by children under the age of six.

For the first few runs, they use Soviet-manufactured sleighs. Then when these collapse under them, they put into operation improvised sledges, using suitcase tops or dustbin lids. Or else they coast down on their bottoms, taking advantage of the dozens of layers of winter clothing they have been wrapped in by over-solicitous parents.

Soviets fail to understand how English adults seem to get more edification from stealing kiddies' cardboard-box sleds and tobogganing down hills, than from a visit to the House Museum of V. I. Lenin. They can only put it down to too much inbreeding among the aristocratic families we all come from.

8 · Eating out

In the West, we eat out for two reasons:

1 for an evening of luxurious intimacy with a loved one fostered by candlelight and unobtrusive waiters;
2 to impress other people with the size of our expense accounts.

The Soviets go to restaurants for the following reasons:

1 a huge loud drunken carousal.

This is partly to do with the lack of savoury bars and discos in the USSR (the restaurant doubles up as both), and partly to do with the mere handful of generations which separates modern-day Soviets from the Khans.

WHERE TO GO

Just as we welcome the siting of American forward hamburger installations on British soil, so the choice of food available in the USSR is tied up with international relations. The range of cuisines served up in Soviet restaurants is determined not on *gastronomic* but on *politico-ideological* grounds. You can enjoy regional delicacies from the fifteen Soviet Socialist Republics, as well as national specialities from throughout the Socialist World. Even Chinese and Yugoslav restaurants operate: a clear indication that the Maoist and Titoist heresies are not taken too seriously by the policy-makers in the Soviet Ministry of Food.

By virtue of being the First City of Socialism, Moscow has arrogated to itself the right to use the least imagination in the naming of its restaurants. Thus, its Hungarian restaurant is called the Budapest, its German Democratic restaurant the Berlin, etc. Once these obvious names have been patented, other cities are forced to delve deep into the atlas for inspiration. Provincial restaurants end up being called after such dubious centres of gastronomy as Leipzig and Potsdam, or else after rivers or mountain ranges.

So blasé gourmets do not have to trek across half the globe to seek out the new 'taste experience' of Turkmen and Tadzhik cuisines. You need go no further than the 'national restaurants' in Moscow, where you can sample these specialities in convivial ethnic surroundings. The Baku is full of extremely prosperous Azerbaijanis; the Uzbekistan is packed with cotton farm administrators on business trips from Tashkent sipping the only green tea in the capital.

There are no vegetarian restaurants. To abstain from meat has peculiar resonances for Russians: it smacks of the obscurantism of the *Old Believers* religious sect, which proclaimed non-meat days to commemorate Christ's suffering on the cross. Nowadays, under Scientific Atheism, wilful abnegation of the main source of protein is considered the height of ingratitude – of which only the most spoilt children of the bourgeoisie are thought capable.

How to get in

In the West, the customer with a reservation enjoys a certain privileged status. In the Soviet Union, however, all men are equal, and people with reservations stand out in the snow with everybody else unless they have mastered the basic techniques of circumventing petty officialdom.

Familiarize yourself with the following routine for gaining entrance to a restaurant, and you will appreciate why in the Soviet Union regular or influential customers prefer to be admitted privately through the staff entrance at the rear.

The doorman

All restaurants have a sign on the door, which may be turned to read either 'closed' or 'no free places'. In its latter state the text should be interpreted *not* as 'no unoccupied places', but rather as 'no gratis places'.

The unquestioned authority of The Sign is backed up by the *doorman*. Originally a sinecure instigated to involve senior citizens in everyday life (and avoid the expense of looking after them in retirement homes), the role of the doorman has now become crucial in determining the smooth running, or complete standstill, of most public institutions.

Remember that the doorman is invariably a war veteran, who probably saw service beating off German panzer divisions at Stalingrad. It is inevitable, therefore, that he will have retained something of the 'they shall not pass' attitude.

A complex procedure is required to negotiate this major obstacle:

1 push your way brazenly through crowd milling outside front door;
2 taking no notice of sign proclaiming 'no free places', tap politely on glass door;
3 tap harder with slight irritation – aware of smug glances and sniggers exchanged by other people in queue;
4 knock firmly at door;
5 doorman limps into view, points irritably to sign and disappears;
6 amidst general mockery, kick viciously at door and yell obscenities;
7 doorman reappears, shaking head disapprovingly;
8 remove rouble note from wallet and show it surreptitiously to doorman;
9 doorman pretends not to notice;
10 add another rouble; crinkle them sensuously;
11 note his disdainful and contemptuous look: 'I cannot be bought' (. . . for so small an amount);
12 repeat 10;
13 the doorman is bought.

You are whisked into a plush, warm and surprisingly empty restaurant.

The cloakroom attendant (*garderobshchitsa*);

In the West, living as we are through the death throes of Capitalism, the cloakroom attendant has become practically obsolete. Bourgeois diners, in constant fear of a spontaneous uprising of the proletariat, prefer to retain coats and bags and sit at their tables huddled up in little cocoons of private property.

In the Soviet Union it is a hideous offence to attempt to enter the dining room until you have handed in to the cloakroom attendant every personal possession except the clothes you stand up in. Should you make as if to pass directly through to the dining room in possession of undeclared goods (hat, umbrella, hunting stick, etc.), the *maître d'hôtel* will herd you straight back to the stern rebukes of the *garderobshchitsa*.

The unquestioned authority of The Sign is backed up by the doorman . . .

You may be forgiven for feeling that this is another example of a code of etiquette invented for the sole purpose of giving other people an excuse to upbraid you.

Great value is set on all work without discrimination in the USSR, and the occupation of cloakroom attendant is considered no less worthy than that of a brain surgeon. In fact, due to the extreme age of the *garderobshchitsa*, a single operation takes a similar amount of time. The elderly attendant tires very quickly from lugging enormous winter greatcoats to and fro and straining on tiptoe to hang them up. So her working day is punctuated by long periods of rest and recuperation – leafing through *Soviet Woman* out of bellowing range of impatient clients.

Over years of experience of causing inconvenience, the cloakroom attendant has perfected many methods of retarding the customer's progress to the dining room. Clothing is refused on a host of technicalities (missing coat hook, torn sleeve, etc.). Arguing one's coat's case with the attendant is seen as special pleading, and usually provokes a recurrence of her hearing problem.

Restaurant service

In the West one makes certain assumptions about service which do not hold true in the Soviet Union:

1 In a Western restaurant a diner purchases his prestige. All the staff realize that you will sign an Access Card slip for an extortionate sum at the end of the evening. So, provided that your accent and the cut of your clothes are right, you will get abundant subservience on credit from the moment you enter the building.

It is, however, futile to think of a Soviet restaurant as an integrated unit. As you have already found out to your cost, cash is required in advance, and each department must be wooed separately.

2 Everyone knows that in an English restaurant there is no real material difference between a cheap meal and an expensive meal. The surplus is made up entirely in grovelling by the waiter. For £5 you get a steak; for £20 you get a steak plus the waiter's human dignity.*

* An example of the reciprocity of this principle is seen in certain cheap Chinese restaurants in Soho. In this permanent saturnalia, there is the feeling that the prices are so low as to be effectively subsidized. The loss is recouped by a role reversal – waiters are immensely rude to customers.

Customers verify that they are getting their money's worth by putting the waiter's unquestioning servility to the test: specifying absurdly elaborate methods of preparation, petulantly sending back to the kitchens perfectly good dishes ... The well-trained waiter does not so much as flinch at this nasty, spoiled behaviour, but, tugging his forelock and murmuring polite apologies for his miserable existence, indulges the customer's every caprice.

Soviet waiters are a different breed altogether. They fall into two classes:

1 *The alarmingly familiar* This type will seat himself at your table and, waving aside the formality of conveying your orders to the kitchen, will strike up a conversation on pertinent issues of the day: how much does a waiter earn in England, is it true that Led Zeppelin have split up, etc.

2 *The sullen and indifferent* Distinguished for his complete lack of respect for the fact that you are paying through the nose for this experience. Entirely spurns qualities that you have come to expect from waiters: viz. civility (i.e. sycophancy) and friendliness (i.e. flattery). Unlike his Western counterpart who is contemptuous only of the poor, the Soviet waiter scorns all his customers without discrimination.

Your visit to a restaurant is part of your initiation process into Socialist norms – designed to teach you that, just because you have the greenbacks, it doesn't mean you call all the shots. Any attempt on your part to invoke a master/servant relationship with any of the staff will be treated as a clear-cut case of 'man's exploitation of man'.

Choosing a table

Do not, upon entering the dining room, make straight for the nearest or most desirably situated table. Restaurants operate very strict demarcation zones, with each waiter being assigned to specific tables. Should the waiter who attends to your table be off-duty that evening, the rest of the staff will allow you to sit there undisturbed all night. You are advised to put yourself into the hands of the *maître d'hôtel*, who, at the slightest show of presumptuousness on your part, will seat you at a table still cluttered with the remnants of the last customer's meal.

Your waiter then approaches and hands you a menu. In his disapproving glower, he seems tacitly to accuse you of having made the mess on your table in the first place. In a rare model of Socialist efficiency, he will return within the minute to take your order. Naturally you are not yet ready. Taking this as a personal rebuff, or as an indication that you are not in fact hungry but just want to sit around for a few hours in the debris of someone else's dinner, he will disappear indefinitely. This will give you ample opportunity to study the *menu*.

Ordering from the menu

The menu should not be taken as a practical guide to the fare available. Like all other Soviet literature it fulfils an *ideologico-propagandistic role*. It is a boast – a showcase of all dishes so far devised by Soviet cuisine. One can feast one's eyes on a wide range of exotic foods: tender cuts of meat blended and flavoured with fragrant spices from the East, served with rich fruits and vegetables harvested on the banks of the Caspian Sea. When it comes to ordering, one is advised to adopt a less wistful frame of mind.

The process of ordering is conducted like a game of Twenty Questions, with the following house rules; *repeat the following sequence indefinitely*:

1 The *customer* selects an item from the menu.
2 The *waiter* indicates briefly that the desired dish is not available.*

This is an invaluable exercise for students of Russian wishing to brush up on the use of the quantitive genitive in negative expressions. The hungry diner, on the other hand, may not wish to use his full allocation of guesses, preferring to pass directly to the second stage of the game:

3a (*impatient*) To ask: 'Well, what *do* you have?'

Attempting to bypass the menu is cheating and spoils all the waiter's fun. He responds by gesturing at the awesome collection of falsehoods in your hand, indicating that you should continue with your guesses.

3b (*sly*) To ask: 'What do you *recommend*?'

---

* The *waiter* at no stage offers excuses or apologies for the absence of requested dishes. Rather, he answers throughout in a brusque and irritable manner, as though you were stupid not to know.
Clue: dishes listed without prices are entirely fictitious.

At this the waiter will take offence – as you have clearly impugned the world standing of Soviet cuisine by suggesting that any of its dishes might be substandard. He will proudly reply 'Vse khoroshi' (they're all good).

Ordering your meal (method two)

Those who wish to break their fast before midnight, and find this process of elimination a tiresome preliminary to getting fed, will resort to the following alternative.

The *maître d'hôtel* shows you to your table and, as he holds your chair out for you, respectfully inquires how much money you have on your person. Using this figure as a working budget, adjusted to allow for the serving staff's handling charge, the kitchen lets loose on you a tide of hors d'oeuvres, main courses and side orders whose existence seems to have eluded the compilers of the menu. The waiters are so busy weighing down your table with succulent, delicately-spiced, ethnic left-overs that they forget to keep you abreast of the fast-increasing running total – and, in the course of one evening, they manage to get through your venture capital for the entire holiday.

Choosing a drink with your meal

In the West, the life of a gastronome can be highly stressful:

1 You are obliged to go through the tiresome ritual of poring painstakingly over the wine list, discussing with your partner the credentials of every particular vintage, and agonizing over the names of chateaux and proprietors – before opting for the most expensive bottle.
2 Throughout the meal you are expected to make lavish pronouncements about the nose and breeding of the wine, and to come up with ludicrous adjectives to describe it.

Being a gourmet in the USSR is infinitely more straightforward. Soviets do not pretend to be equipped with refined palates that can taste a wine's bottle age, or sophisticated nostrils that can smell the width and direction of the vine rows. All gastronomic considerations are subverted to a more important end: getting drunk as quickly as possible.

This set of priorities informs the traditional Russian way of drinking. Whatever the alcohol – classic vintages cultivated in the Transcarpathian mountains, sparkling and dessert wines gently warmed on the southern slopes of the Caucasus, or finely-distilled spirits from the vodka factories of Kharkov – it is poured neat into a tumbler and gulped down in one.

Which wine to order

The whole notion of choosing a wine whose flavour complements that of the food is redundant in the Soviet Union for two reasons:

1 As demented Russian etiquette demands that everything be downed in one, no *drink* is ever tasted. Because of this,
2 By the time the *food* arrives, you are too drunk to taste that either.

In order to impress your companions with your sophistication, you need only order the following drinks:

Champagne Despite its glamorous heritage, champagne enjoys no special exemption status. It may not be sniffed, sipped, or rolled around the tongue, but *must* be tipped unceremoniously down the throat, like any other alcohol.

This cavalier treatment comes as a refreshing contrast to Western customs. In the Soviet Union, champagne, the most prestigious and pricey item on the menu, is ordered, *not* on the pretence that the wine buff has such a sensitive palate that he can appreciate only the most delicate of flavours, but – quite blatantly – because it is the most prestigious and pricey item on the menu.

Vodka This is drunk because it never occurs to Russians *not* to drink vodka on social occasions.

Soviets take their vodka very seriously, and pride themselves on being vodka buffs. This is strange, given two factors:

1 vodka is deliberately distilled so as to be colourless, odourless and tasteless;
2 vodka is consumed in such a peremptory way as to bypass all sensory organs.

As far as Westerners can make out, the only difference between vodka brands is the colour of the label. Apart from this, vodka conforms to the basic egalitarian nature of its country of production: all brands are equally horrible.

Throughout the meal vodka toasts must be drunk, neat and in one, in strict rotation with champagne toasts. Amateur sociologists may remark on this bizarre combination to be found at the Russian table of the most *aristocratic* and the most *proletarian* of beverages. However, it is the mixing of the *drinks*, rather than the ideologies, that the diner is apt to find most alarming.

The waiter is extremely assiduous about serving you drink – for which you pay cash-on-delivery. During the course of your meal, you may become dimly aware of the following:

1 *untoward price fluctuations*   e.g. the price of the champagne with which the waiter is plying you tends to increase in direct proportion to your blood alcohol level
2 *diminishing relative potency of the vodka*   lest you overdo it and spoil your evening, the waiter serves you carafes of diluted house spirits, levying a small surcharge for this precautionary service.

Entertainment

At seemingly random intervals throughout your meal you will be entertained by the *house band* – a seedy pack of middle-aged men, who, having paid their dues, clearly now feel it is time to extract compensation from their audience. As Soviet contracts are rather more durable than their fickle, renegotiable English equivalents, the band are probably well into the second decade of their residency, and may have neglected to update their material. Though the vocalist is often reluctant to commit himself to a known European language, this material is likely to be largely Soviet. Certain more contemporary Western numbers may also qualify for inclusion in the repertoire, but only on grounds of outstanding blandness (e.g. 'Hello', 'I just called to say I love you', etc.).

As the only concession to the eighties, the combo's formidable capacity for causing unpleasantness has recently been enhanced by the Soviet invention of the *synthesizer*. This instrument appears to have only one setting, 'offensive rasp', which the keyboard player uses with great gusto.

The Western concept of the 'set' (that is, a period of an hour or more during which the band is continually playing) does not appear to have gained widespread acceptance in the Soviet Union. Instead, the band's appearances on stage are extremely sporadic – subject to some supra-Hegelian laws and, out of respect for Socialist norms, wholly independent of public opinion.

Should they manage a sustained stay, you may be surprised to observe hep-cat admirals in full regalia jitterbugging with their portly wives alongside 'young people' in pressed Levis. In this sense the dance floor is truly internationalist, with all generations and races united by a common bond of tastelessness, gyrating energetically to crass renditions of Demis Roussos hits and Armenian folk songs.

For a small fee, the band will play any request you make – provided it is not so modern as to have post-dated their repertoire. Occasionally some carouser will begin throwing five-rouble notes at the stage, getting the band to play the same song several times in succession. This forces the other dancers into a time-space continuum distortion, left repeating the same steps over and over again with mounting self-consciousness. Eventually they retire grumpily to the edge of the dance-floor, leaving the tune-caller to sway moronically on his own, like an unwanted suitcase at baggage reclaim.

WARNING Dostoevsky stresses the Russians' morbid love of degradation; Lenin spoke of their instinctive striving towards the collective. As a result, the *Birdie Dance*, which allows them to fulfil both these yearnings at the same time, is gruesomely popular. What was merely an embarrassing fad in England has become a national institution in the Soviet Union, and is performed on all social occasions. It is imperative, therefore, to keep a low profile whenever you hear the melody being struck up, otherwise you will be dragged on to the dance floor and required to instruct a pack of Kalmucks in this ritual humiliation.

Your only prospect of salvation lies in the hope that the Birdie Dance will be rendered obsolete by the arrival of *Agadoo* in the Soviet Union in the mid 1990s. However it is possible that the latter abomination may not find favour with the proletariat due to its obscure references to bourgeois luxury goods (pineapple, coffee).

Payment

Though the current miserable exchange rate has put them more or less on a par, roubles sometimes add up differently from pounds. Indeed, under certain unscrupulous circumstances, six or seven roubles may conspire together to make as many as ten. The bill is often the only example of inflation in the otherwise stable Soviet economy; unquestioning payment of it may amount to leaving a 250 per cent gratuity to the staff.

The bill's tendency towards unrestricted growth is due to the following features:

1 Whatever is being celebrated (wedding, 'cotton' anniversary,* divorce†), there is a single aim: to get utterly blotto. The vodka and champagne team up to bring about prompt erasure of all memory of the occasion. In the absence of any other record of the event, the only way to gauge how much you enjoyed yourself is by seeing how out of pocket you are the next morning.

The waiter obliges you by throwing in the cost of a few extra dinners, and charging you for a handful of absent friends – endowing the festivity with a retrospective grandeur and bloating his personal fortune.

2 *Tipping*   At the time of the Great October Socialist Revolution, waiters paraded down the streets of Moscow, with banners proclaiming: 'Waiters of the world, unite! We reject the demeaning, patronizing practice of tipping!' Modern-day waiters do not feel the need to prove themselves by such gestures, and feel a certain awkwardness about the ideological extremism of their more radical forebears.

The waiter appreciates, however, that you may feel uncomfortable about tipping, and relieves you of the embarrassment by including his gratuity as an invisible item in your bill. As middleman between the kitchens and your table, he feels uniquely qualified to judge the quality of the service, and awards himself a percentage accordingly.

Should you suspect any irregularities, you may demand the *complaints book*. This is a symbolic act designed to bring recalcitrant waiters to heel. The customer does not actually expect the waiter to rush obligingly off and fetch the means to his own denunciation; in fact, no one has ever seen a complaints book. It is merely a metaphysical concept designed to keep people in line and encourage productivity – rather like Communism or the Dictatorship of the Proletariat. Rest assured that the merest invocation of its name will produce a satisfactory show of reverence.

---

* *Cotton anniversary*   first wedding anniversary.
† Few people get past the second of these before celebrating the third.

Guide to eating out

1 UPMARKET: *SHVEDSKY STOL*

As an alternative to the traditional sit-down meal the hotel may offer a *shvedsky stol* (Swedish table). This is a microcosm of Communism, pioneered in an experimental form in hotels, using foreigners as guinea pigs.* Displayed on large tables is a mixed hot and cold buffet: for a down payment of four roubles, you are theoretically entitled to take as many helpings as you can bear.

Regrettably, the experiment fails. Marx's rash prediction that under such circumstances the enlightened proletariat would *not* stuff themselves until they were ill is fully refuted. Each takes according to his greed, ending up with piles of food left uneaten on the plate and a stomach in a state of revolutionary turmoil.

In the meantime, the authorities have implemented measures to accommodate this gourmandise:

1 The serving women act as a powerful deterrent to gluttony. After the blatantly hostile and contemptuous glare that greets you the *first* time you go up, only customers with an iron will (and matching stomach) will wish to run the gauntlet of the serving counter for a second helping.

2 The system reabsorbs all surplus food: Russian dishes· are specifically designed to be self-perpetuating. Whatever you leave on your plate is reincorporated into the salad or soup it came from, and served up to the next customer.

---

*Just in case of total failure, the blame for this system is fobbed off on the Swedes – to punish that nation for years of concerted neutrality and humourlessness. We in Britain do much the same thing with a rather dull and unappetizing vegetable.

Inspired by the fast food establishments pioneered in the USA, the Soviets have instituted their own special equivalent. A triumph of Soviet rationalization, the *stolovaya* has banished all the good qualities of its American prototype (efficiency, friendliness, colourful décor), and conserved all the bad ones (horrible food).

Stolovaya literally means 'dining room' and staff make a conscious effort to recreate the informal atmosphere of the family dinner table; they are especially fond of *huge blazing rows*.

Aware that society can develop only as a result of the struggle between the *contradictions within society itself*, the serving women supplement their nominal duties (dishing out food, taking money) with the vocational, and highly ideologically credible, task of *agitation*. Exhibiting remarkable manipulative skills, they:

1 force the customer at the head of the queue to make a stand on basic consumer rights by maliciously withholding dishes;
2 whip up opposition to the dissenter among other queuers being inconvenienced by the delay;
3 having precipitated the revolutionary situation in the queue, saunter off to the kitchens for lengthy discussions on the fulfilment of soup production norms.

Menu

One may choose between the set meal and ordering from the à la carte menu. For technical reasons the two are usually indistinguishable and run as follows:

> 200 ml soup
> beef Stroganoff/bifshteks
> 100 g vermicelli
> fruit drink
> fruit compote
> 150 ml tea
> bread

Notes on menu

1 The *stolovaya* can lay claim to the invention of a dish which has not yet been picked up on by Western caterers: *molochny sup* (milk soup).

Before you tuck into this culinary anomaly – a bowl of lukewarm milk with a globule of fat in the middle – pause to reflect on the collective sanity of any nation which chooses to make a soup out of an item which is already liquid.

2 Considering that internationally recognized Russian dishes should be a protected species, Soviet chefs are remarkably cavalier about their preparation. The lapsing of the Stroganoff estate has democratically allowed the name to grace any dog-ear of meat with gravy, while 'bifshteks' – fried meat patty swathed in gravy – bears no resemblance whatsoever to beefsteaks living or dead.

3 The only difference between the fruit drink (beverage) and the fruit compote (dessert) is that the second thin brown liquid allows you to get in some practice at mandarin-bobbing by including a piece of marinated fruit.

4 Black rye bread is a compulsory side-order with any meal in the Soviet Union. Thus, if, out of courtesy to your effete and pampered Western stomach, you try to avoid taking any, the cashier will bully you into doing so. If you then don't eat it, you will find yourself in contravention of a large notice on the wall which gravely informs you: 'Bread is our national wealth – do not waste it.'

Things to do (3)

OVERNIGHT TRAIN

Train routes in the Soviet Union have exotic names. The *Red Arrow* speeds the seven hundred kilometres between Hero-Cities Moscow and Leningrad. The *Russia* is the trans-Siberian run, dashing across steppe, tundra and virgin forest all the way to Khabarovsk.

'Lara's Theme' rings in your ears as you trudge across the snowbound platform to reach your stout wooden carriage. It is presumed that the engines are now universally diesel, though no tourist, to the authors' knowledge, has ever walked the mile-long length of the train to ascertain this for sure.

Conditions

While the hardier provincials take up places in the traditional *hard* compartments (open carriages where whole families bed down on wooden benches), you, as a Westerner, will be allotted a *soft* (i.e. first class) berth in a four-sleeper compartment that admirably recreates the over-crowded squalor of Soviet urban existence.

This cosy box may well turn into a Sartrean chamber, as you find yourself incarcerated with two voluble Collective Farm managers intent on improving their English, and a woman who retires primly to bed immediately the train sets off.

NB: No Snoring compartments cannot be guaranteed.

Personnel

The conductress – a hefty woman in a blue brass-buttoned uniform and a silly hat – is responsible for the implementation of Socialist Discipline. She prowls down the corridor, sliding back compartment doors to make sure that the Party's anti-alcohol measures are being adhered to. She exiles smokers to the airless passageway between the carriages, where the risk to one's lungs is compounded by the hazards of standing above two viciously clashing bumpers.

At eleven o'clock she interrupts those merrily chatting in the corridor with barked instructions to go to bed at once. Should any persist in disturbing the peace, she returns ten minutes later, with her decree backed up by stout conductresses from neighbouring carriages.

The journey

Out of a slavish devotion to speed at all costs, trains in the West pelt blindly into the night towards their destination, eventually turfing their bleary-eyed passengers on to deserted station platforms at four in the morning. Trains in the Soviet Union follow a more sensible timetable: they always depart at 11 p.m. and reach their destination at 7 a.m.

Russian geography stubbornly refuses to submit itself to Soviet rationalization. In view of the disproportionate distances between different cities, a strict adherence to the timetable sometimes involves the train ambling along at walking pace for much of the journey and making inordinately long stops at through stations.

These hour long standstills can prove extremely distressing for those passengers who have contravened the Party's ban on drinking, for toilets are locked and strictly out of bounds when the train is stationary. Should you be found occupying the toilet at the approach of one of these stops, the indignant conductress will break and enter with a master key and forcibly eject you.

At three in the morning you are jolted awake to find the train standing at a floodlit station. A huge voice booms out of the loudspeaker; vast numbers of soldiers are running up and down. In your somnolent state you hazily conclude that war has been declared, and that you are about to suffer the ultimate irony of being incinerated by the NATO weapons into which you have so enthusiastically pumped your Inland Revenue contributions for so long. After waiting for a full bleary four minutes, you presume that the station is not located in a first strike area and take the opportunity to snatch a little more shut-eye before the holocaust.

During the day, on the longer routes, whenever you stop at a station in the provinces, you will see hordes of the local peasantry mounting the train with bundles of goods. Snap out of your

Zhivagoesque daydreams: they are not *kulaks* fleeing the Bolshevik advance, carrying off their possessions. They are just giving you a chance to sample the local agricultural produce. Capitalizing on the buffet car's failure to stock anything but chicken, they pass up and down the corridors, selling their wares: apples, berries, nasty greasy fry-ups of onion and potato wrapped in newspaper.

Arrival

Your arrival is heralded by a fanfare of trumpets: at six o'clock the in-built radio starts up, piping a rousing rendition of the Soviet national anthem into each slumbering compartment. As you fumble blindly to turn it off, the conductress comes in to shake you awake and provide you with the passenger's one democratic entitlement in this autocratic microcosm – a cup of tea. As the radio is now well into the weather forecast for Kazakhstan, you rouse yourself and observe the stirring sight of the industrial plants and high-rise housing estates on the outskirts of your destination. To deter this minor relaxation, the conductress returns almost immediately to snatch the bedlinen from under you.

As the train pulls in, everyone is filled with sudden energy and surges forward simultaneously, blocking the corridor with their luggage. If you are tempted to sit it out smugly and wait till the commotion is over, be warned: within three minutes of arrival, without any warning, the train is shunted off into sidings several kilometres down the line, taking with it all persons or baggage not previously removed.

PART THREE

Introduction

Part Two has furnished you with the skills necessary for basic material survival in the Soviet Union. You are now fully equipped, for example, to bribe your way into public buildings, be defrauded in elegant restaurants, and get irretrievably lost in *any* Soviet town.

But a full understanding of Soviet life requires a further level of awareness – how to cope with Soviet *people*.

After a lifelong exposure to Western media, you have a fixed notion of the USSR as composed entirely of octogenarians in greatcoats reviewing parades of military hardware. It may come as something of a surprise to you that the Soviet Union contains any *people* at all.

In fact, the monolithic Heroic-Soviet-People-Builder-of-Communism comprises 270 million individuals. It is a nation of extraordinary diversity – urbanite, peasant; worker, intellectual; Russian, Ukrainian, Khanty-Manty; bilious, hypersensitive . . .

Conveniently, Marxism–Leninism has pruned everything down to a manageable level by abolishing spurious class distinctions. Contemporary Soviet society breaks down into two distinct types, both of whom take a deep interest in your movements now that you have started getting around on your own:

1 the *unofficial*, who are avid to solicit information and opinions from the decadent West;
2 the *official*, who are anxious to prevent the dissemination of information and opinions from the decadent West.

With this etiquette guide in hand, you should be able to identify these types straightaway and alter your behaviour accordingly.

Note In the Eastern and Southern Republics, where foreigners rarely stray, you may not be accorded special treatment when you reveal that you are English. Those locals who have actually *heard* of

England automatically assume that you are a flash Estonian trying it on. Others, only dimly aware of the existence of foreign countries, often believe that England is an Autonomous Soviet Socialist Republic.

9 · Speculation

Though Marxist theory denies the need for it, and the Soviet Criminal Code expressly forbids it, the petty economic crime of *speculation** persists in the USSR. In urban agglomerations throughout the Soviet Union, black marketeers (*fartsovshchiki*) make a living by trading in foreign goods. This has presented the authorities with a problem.

On the one hand, speculation constitutes a grave crime against Socialism, a flagrant contravention of the Leninist call for spiritual betterment, and an intolerably easy way to rake off vast personal profits.

On the other, these characters are far too disreputable to hold down a proper job anyway. Indeed, from the ideological point of view, it is quite useful to have a few of them around: the unedifying sight of them, as they scurry obsessively round pestering foreigners and propositioning them for their belongings, is enough to warn any vacillating citizen off the follies of private enterprise.

So the Party lets this anti-social minority go about its illegal business, satisfying itself with a permanent propaganda offensive against parasites in general and the occasional execution of big-time speculators in particular. In the meantime, it is content to accept the odd charitable contribution from the private sector, payable directly to one of the State's representatives (i.e. arresting officer, judge, Party high-up).

The Soviet system places great importance on companionship, and the Westerner will rarely find himself without a Soviet 'fellow traveller'. On those infrequent occasions when your guide is not on hand to furnish you with fascinating insights into the exact

* With the approach of Communism, many types of crime common in the West have been eradicated in the USSR. Computer fraud, for example, does not exist in the Soviet Union – but then neither does computer hardware.

dimensions of local revolutionary eyesores, a stream of alternative escorts will be provided.

As you emerge from your hotel, drinking in the sweet air of independence, a moustachioed figure in standard issue uniform of green parka and Adidas bag will sidle up to you and hiss conspiratorially: 'Speak English . . ?' The more romantically inclined should note that this is not the KGB recruitment officer handing out long-term leases on penthouse flats in Odessa in exchange for details of NATO forward defence installations. Rather, it is the first in a chain of Soviet 'Minder' extras who dog the Westerner's footsteps.

An exchange of ritual code words follows. The speculator prompts you with 'English? Bobby Charlton . . ? Margaret Tetcher . . ? Jeans . . ? Sony Walkman . . ? Dollars . . ?', to which you make the correct cryptic responses: ' . . . er . . . yes . . . no thank you . . . no . . . go away please . . .'.

A contact has now been made (as far as he is concerned) and he will follow you for miles, propositioning you on various scores, as you attempt to sound off about Byzantine architecture and the Russian soul. If, finding this courtship rather tiresome, you try to deter his attentions with a brusque 'No', you will only encourage him further: every refusal is taken as an example of hard-nosed bargaining on your part. He will respond by upping his offer, or by transferring his attentions to some other, more preposterous and impractical item – your camera, shoes, the shirt off your back. Alternatively, he may woo the foreign currency section of your wallet with offers of lucrative exchange rates.

HOW TO DETER STREET SPECULATORS

The only way to deter street speculators is to decrease radically your market value in their eyes. As their first question is inevitably 'Where are you from?' (to determine how affluent/fashionable/gullible you are), the artful tourist will answer in one of two ways:

1 By pretending to be from a Soviet Baltic Republic/Brother Socialist country. Watch the speculator's obsequity turn into virulent abuse in mid-sentence. However, besides being anathema to your pride, there is an attendant danger in voluntarily assuming the identity of an ethnic minority in the Soviet Union. Although the USSR is a harmonious union of fraternal republics, untainted by

racialism, the Russians have been known to enter into occasional misunderstandings which leave their Baltic brethren without the use of certain vital internal organs.

2 By claiming as your Motherland a bourgeois country of such international insignificance that even the Soviets hold it in contempt.

This is more difficult than you might think. Even countries like Luxembourg and Wales, although paltry nonentities by Western European standards (in terms of population size and annual budget deficit), are still decadent capitalist states, hotbeds of imperialistic revanchism, and as such greatly revered by the Soviet criminal underworld.

The only country of absolutely no economic interest to the Soviet Union is *Greenland*, its principal assets being ice and a miserable populace, both of which the Soviets have in large supply. The black marketeer will veer away blankly if you confront him with this name, as he has never heard of it.

Once he has positively identified you as a Westerner, neither artfully woven disinformation, nor your evident unwillingness to have anything to do with him, are likely to deter your *fartsovshchik*, as he is mesmerized by your clothing, and extremely stupid into the bargain. He will continue to harass you with inane bonhomie about fashion accessories and one-hit wonders from the early seventies. This will leave you no other solution than to seek sanctuary in your hotel, taking refuge behind the garrison of doormen.

Abandoned on the threshold of the hotel, suffering the harangues of an indignant doorman, your speculator feels bereft. His passions aroused, his mind unusually stirred and buzzing with foreign exchange calculations, he is left with a feeling of frustration, of having been betrayed by somebody whom he has come to regard as a close friend. Your behaviour strikes him as all the more churlish, given your contributory negligence in flaunting your Western finery all around town.

Provoked into action, your speculator goes through a speedy transformation from oafish slob to clear-headed tactician. He mobilizes all his *khloptsy** – a motley crowd of disreputables who pass for experts in certain fields of minority trading (Village People albums, leg-warmers, etc.). He posts them all around the hotel, so that each exit is guarded by a dishevelled sentry in a Pink Floyd T-shirt.

* *Khlopets* (coll. Ukrainian): **1** (fig.) = 'mate'; **2** (literal) = 'complete dolt'

A motley crowd of disreputables.

Forced to sit out the blockade in your room, you will be pestered every five minutes by phonecalls offering you an honourable surrender and an absurd rendezvous by the obelisk in Victory Square. Worn down by this war of attrition, you mutter agreement, and finally emerge – waving a pair of jeans as a token of submission.

INFORMAL VISIT TO CONTACT'S FLAT

Now that your contact has succeeded in winning your confidence, as well as a percentage of your trading rights, you will receive an invitation to his flat. This will be an edifying experience, with your status being somewhere between that of visiting royalty and an exhibit on 'The Price is Right'. The whole family assembles to eye up your belongings and give an evaluative squeeze to your clothing as you pass.

You may be taken by surprise by your host's opening conversational gambit: without frittering away any time in pleasantries he makes a point-blank demand for your Lonsdale sweatshirt.

You should under no circumstances offer to *give* him the desired item. It is not that his pride will be offended in accepting a gift, nor that he has any inherent love of haggling; merely, that he will take you for a complete mug, and, however deep the personal ties between you, proceed to clean you out. He will not be polite and mutter 'No no I mustn't I couldn't possibly', etc. He *can* and *will* – and then, without taking time out to be grateful, will follow up with a bid for your boots . . . sadly unaware that the only pleasure the English get from spontaneous generosity is all the grovelling gratitude it engenders in the recipient.

As you begin to wise up, he varies the ploys:

1 He dresses up his subsequent demand for your *jeans* as a request for 'something to remember you by'. This adept play on your sympathies may stop you from spotting the logical flaw: that, if he wants a souvenir of you, why does he ask for something which fails to distinguish you from a billion other Westerners?

2 Eventually, in order to maintain the respect of your friend and your own solvency, you too begin to haggle. This brings out the true resourcefulness of your Soviet acquaintance. He begins by denigrating your brand-new Levis, frowning and shaking his head at the poor quality of the workmanship. Despite this, he will deign to take them off your hands, 'so that you don't have to drag them around

town with you'. Then, professing complete ignorance of black market cost indexes, he offers you a token sum for them. You discover later, upon further acquaintance with the private sector, that he made an extremely shrewd investment, yielding 300 per cent dividend on the purchase.

3 Loath to encumber you with excess roubles, he may try to offset his purchase with an exchange in kind. As he has developed an absurd craving for tasteless clothing from your country (blue jeans, Adidas trainers, etc.), he hopes that perhaps you have developed an equally absurd craving for tasteless clothing from *his* (Ukrainian embroidered shirts, Estonian knitwear, military greatcoat). Be aware when negotiating such an exchange that the former items come extremely cheap in the USSR, and the latter may well be confiscated by customs officials when you leave.

TIPS ON SOVIET FASHION – FOR PROSPECTIVE TRADERS

(*a*) Though the time difference between Britain and the Soviet Union ranges from three to fourteen hours, the fashion lag is anywhere from two years (in the large Europeanized capitals) to two hundred years (in closed towns, tundra, etc.).

Aware of the transient nature of most Western fashions, Soviets do not jump on bandwagons immediately. For a fashion to be popular in the Soviet Union, it must have been tried, tested and preferably obsolete for a decade in the West.

In the more developed cities, however, the Soviet population has evolved from the late-sixties suspended animation which still reigned a few years ago. Early punk and mod styles are favoured by the vanguard of rebellious youth, though they are still quite prepared to pay good money for 'Legalize Cannabis' T-shirts and albums called *The Best of Knebworth*.

(*b*) Jeans are, as ever, the staple currency in the Soviet black economy. In fact the USSR would provide an excellent setting for a Ray Cooney farce, as the Westerner is always in danger of losing his trousers. Soviets exhibit a sound knowledge of Freudian theory that is uncanny in a country where the man's works are banned. When you are publicly propositioned – say, by a waiter in a particularly large and crowded restaurant – it is invariably your trousers that he wants to buy.

(*c*) Soviets insist on guaranteed-quality brands (Levis, Adidas), steering clear of more recent, presumably flash-in-the-pan names (Falmers, Nike). This is not because they are particularly perceptive about quality. Rather, it is that Soviets, conscious of how easy they find it to fleece a friend, are themselves very wary of being ripped off. Unable to retain any but the first brand name they hear, they assume that anything else is a poor-quality imitation.

TABLE OF RELATIVE VALUES

	Western goods	*What Soviets fob you off with in exchange*
1	Levi denims	A large selection of Soviet fur hats (small, medium or large) from a range of home-produced furs – sable, mink or rabbit.
2	*Sergeant Pepper, Dark Side of the Moon* & other pop classics	Christmas food hamper – large pot of Beluga caviare, box of Havana cigars, two jars of conserved red peppers from Hungary.
3	Large portable tape-recorder	A handsome addition to your wardrobe: full dress uniform of the Red Army, with medals from Great Patriotic War campaigns appended.
4	*Animal, Lust* and other after-shave lotions	Top-quality knitted socks, incorporating traditional folk patterns. Made in a cooperative in the Pskov region. (3 roubles 40 kopecks from major stores.)

FURTHER CONTACT WITH SPECULATORS

Tourists about to go to the USSR are warned of possible harassment from the KGB. In fact, the real danger to Westerners lies elsewhere: in the unremitting attentions of street speculators, picking up the scent of your designer-label denims.

1 Should it be approaching the end of your stay, and there be the feeling amongst the Soviets that you have failed to respond adequately to the generosity of your self-appointed guides and hosts (i.e. you have not, blubbing with gratitude, handed over to them the entire contents of your suitcase), you may be invited round for a fateful last supper.

Here you will undergo a metamorphosis similar to that of Cinderella at midnight. Having arrived dressed sprucely in the latest Western fashion, you emerge some hours later with no watch on your wrist, tacking mournfully upwind in a pair of big Soviet flares.*

2 Should this fail, on your day of departure a send-off delegation – comprising friends, contacts and associated marauders – will be dispatched. On arrival at your hotel room, they will be driven into a frenzy that transcends decorum, at the thought of the 500 per cent devaluation that the contents of your suitcase will undergo on crossing the Soviet border. In imitation of their Mongol forebears, they will ransack your luggage, pillaging all remaining items of value.

Out of deference to the general tone of Soviet life, you may have brought with you only dull, colourless clothing. This will not deter your Soviet. Trusting to the taste of Western fashion designers, and having none of his own, he assumes that, if an article of clothing comes from abroad, it must be:

(*a*) tasteful;

(*b*) at all costs prevented from returning thither.

3 In a despairing last fling, as you set off for the airport, the Soviet may invite you to perform a ritual exchange of garments – rather like footballers swapping shirts at the end of a match. He relieves you of your Hepworths pure wool overcoat; you get a green padded worker's coat (*vatnik*), which, he assures you in a convincingly cautious whisper, is a Siberian convict's jacket. This may or may not be – what is more likely to concern you is that it *looks* like a horrible quilted waistcoat purchased from Mister Buyrite by a distant ancestor.

HOW TO ATTRACT SPECULATORS

In certain Soviet towns (e.g. the Hero-Cities in the western republics), you can wander around freely without being accosted by speculators. This is not so much because, through a combination of

---

* Certain observers, who mistakenly ascribe some modicum of taste to speculators, are persuaded that such transactions are executed not for profit motives, but for symbolic value: in order to savour the sight of the West humiliated, in genuinely unpleasant and retrogressive legwear.

the ravages of war and the imposition of Socialism, the citizenry has been cowed into a model of uprightness. Rather, it is because these cities, despite boasting daring post-war reconstructions and 20 sq m of verdure per person, are left off most tourists' itineraries. Starved of all contact, and all possible commerce, with the outside world, the local speculators migrate to the more decadent Moscow and Leningrad, or else 'go straight' and take up a position at the tractor factory.

Thus, in these Stalinist backwaters, the regulation Parka and Adidas bag are relatively uncommon sights. Doubtless this will come as a relief to the earnest sightseer, who can go about visiting Great Patriotic War memorials without the slightest intrusion.

However, you may be one of those shrewd foreigners who, in expectation of the inevitable triumph of Communism, wants to invest in the security of roubles. You should be able to do better than the paltry one-for-one rate offered in the hotel. But you will need to take the initiative yourself, to elicit some reaction from the dulled population.

1 Locate a potential *fartsovshchik* – anyone under forty with a modicum of dress sense. Stop them with a spurious inquiry: the way to the House Museum of T. G. Shevchenko. Express yourself in a pronounced American accent: no black marketeer worth his salt wants to encumber himself with slumping pounds sterling.

You may evoke a response from the huddles of pock-marked adolescents who cluster on every Soviet street corner. Attempting to raise their status amongst their peers, they may bravely offer you roubles, though it soon becomes obvious that they are far too gormless to have any.

If you do attract a bona fide speculator, beware: deprived of any commercial dealings since the last tourists passed through three years before, he may try to make a sufficient killing on you to compensate for all the lean months in between. Playing up to the Westerner's desire for the thrills and exotica of crime, he drags you off into a dark corner. Here you find that the ten rouble notes in his deft hands have a miraculous power of turning into one rouble notes in your pocket. Should you appear a little 'green', your contact may take you under his wing and decide that you would rather have the option of doubling your money: in place of a tidy wad of roubles, you may find a few lottery tickets, which, through an oversight, transpire to be two months old.

2 *Visit to the market*   To rouse it from its traditional indolence and awaken it to the glories of Marxism–Leninism, the authorities have galvanized the peasantry by a system of mild economic incentives, allowing it to sell for personal gain all produce grown on private allotments. Agricultural workers have responded to the Party's liberalizing measures with revolutionary zeal, flocking from all over the Soviet Union into the collective farm markets to indulge in this officially-sanctioned speculation.

Georgians and Armenians,* tired of selling melons at a 2000 per cent mark-up, are always eager to diversify (e.g. bulk-buying clothing, electronic equipment, etc.). Therefore, if you yourself wish to get involved in this Soviet experiment in free enterprise, take your liquid assets to the Central Market and seek out the eight-generation-strong regional branch of *Bakunian Brothers*, Bartering and Black Marketeering Chain.

Hardly have you stepped over the threshold than you are accosted by street urchins, who escort you confidently to their uncle's fruit-and-vegetable stall. Through an alarming display of ventriloquism, the stallholder praises his pomegranates in a stentorian voice, while propositioning you about your stock-in-trade under his breath. You hand your jeans over for a routine inspection . . . and watch in vain as they are passed backwards towards the end of the stall, through a hundred outstretched hands testing the quality, size and flare width.

Your merchandise, now safely out of your reach, becomes the focus of fierce debate and frenetic backstage activity. The shrieks and brawls attract the attention of neighbouring stallholders and curious passers-by, who muscle in, in the hope of a spontaneous auction.

The wizened patriarch at the back has finally passed judgement on the value of your jeans and this information is communicated along the ranks of great-uncles and third-cousins.

The cartel's front men begin to bargain. Your final offer is whittled down to a slim percentage and a deal is struck. You then try to persuade the next line of this. Unhampered by the concept of the oral contract, they deny all knowledge of any such agreement and express outrage at the extortionate sum you are demanding.

* *Georgians, Armenians*   Peoples from the Soviet Republics of the Caucasian isthmus. The male of the species is distinguished by its leather jacket, from which protrude a huge gut and a thick black moustache.

You are finally handed a wad of wrinkled banknotes. As you attempt to count them to verify the famous Georgian integrity, the look-out rushes back with a warning about the imminent (and very timely) arrival of the *militsia*. Generations of Georgians disappear in a flash, leaving only the beaming stallholder, who performs a final trample on your dignity by adeptly persuading you to exchange your meagre gains for a half dozen persimmons.

FURTHER SPECULATION

The Soviet Union does wonders for your social magnetism. Not only do you tend to pal up with street speculators, who are prepared to offer you roubles, army uniforms, their undying friendship and other worthless commodities in exchange for Western luxury goods; but you will also find your capacity to attract members of the opposite sex considerably enhanced.

Those tempted by the exoticism of 'having an affair with a native' should maintain a healthy scepticism and be aware of the implications of this kind of casual arrangement in the Soviet Union. In some cases, the Soviet is drawn to the foreigner, *not* because of allure, looks or affinity of character, but rather because of that most attractive of foreign characteristics, the *passport*.

The fetishism of the foreign residency permit is quite widespread a sexual predilection amongst Soviets. Slightly ashamed of this deviant form of sensuality, those who suffer from it are apt to keep it secret from their Western partners, until they are safely married and out of the Soviet Union. Westerners who belatedly learn the true nature of the particular 'je ne sais quoi' which so turned on their Soviet paramours, are usually very hurt and sue for immediate divorce – an outcome which the Soviet, now a British citizen and eligible to receive social security payments, learns to live with.

The rare breed of conscientious speculators will come clean from the start and baldly propose a *fictitious marriage* – a black market transaction dealing in the highest denomination currency: the *exit visa*.

Note   Soviets do not make spurious claims to 'love someone for his soul'. Dialectical Materialism has taught them that it is futile to try to separate a person's nature from the other crucial conditioning forces (i.e. his money, lifestyle, creature comforts, etc.).

131

Book black market

The Soviet Ministry of Culture willingly answers the Soviet people's demand for pamphlets on agronomy, smelting processes and the Leading Role played in them by the Communist Party. The closed economy, however, necessitates the imposition of certain trade restrictions, by means of which the Government can protect its own market. For this reason, all publications not put out by the State Publishing House are placed under a strict embargo.

Some intellectuals, however, suffering from an unfortunate outbreak of curiosity, seek out books which are *not* published under official aegis. These fall into several categories:

(*a*) *Anti-Soviet propaganda*   This is a general term, which covers any book which is not absurdly ingratiating towards the Soviet Union (e.g. the book you are reading now). Any book which neither details the heroic defence of the Motherland against Hitlerite Fascism nor exhorts the population to even greater efforts to advance the cause of Proletarian Internationalism, is deemed unsuitable for the Soviet reading public. Works stimulating the imagination or critical faculties are considered gross slander against the Soviet state. Especially reviled are the virulent defamations disseminated by CIA agents and flunkeys of capital (e.g. Solzhenitsyn, Sakharov).

(*b*) *Religious propaganda*   Though written between 2000 and 3000 years before Marx, the Bible is highly anti-Soviet in character and intent. In its befuddling of the proletariat with mysticism and spirituality, its fragmentation of the collective by its concentration on 'inner life' and the 'individual conscience', it is obscurantist, regressive and seditious.

(*c*) *Zionist propaganda*   After the failure of the Zionist world takeover (documents from the Elders of Zion were cunningly intercepted by the Soviet authorities and are regularly publicized under their auspices), the main thrust of Zionism today is towards Soviet Jews: inveigling them to turn their backs on the-country-which-fed-clothed-and-educated-them and emigrate to Israel. Any books explicitly supporting this imperialist and genocidal ideology, especially Hebrew language textbooks and Isaac Bashevis Singer's short stories, are outlawed.

(*d*) *Pornography*   As Western liberals point out, one of the major infringements on human rights in the Soviet Union is the ban on pornography and 'erotica'. Soviets are deprived of several basic freedoms: to purchase glossy catalogues full of air-brushed pudenda from any newsagents, to enliven their jaded senses by reading about other people's sexual problems in *Forum* magazine, etc.

Book black markets operate on the outskirts of major cities at weekends, in a clearing which doubles up as a boggy marshland for most of the year. The authorities tolerate it, as it gives the anaemic intellectuals who participate in it a chance to get out of their musty archives and get a bit of fresh air into their lungs. The procedure is reminiscent of cruising in Greenwich Village. People parade up and down sporting handwritten signs declaring their particular needs and what they have to offer in exchange (Bulgakov for Dahl volume 4). You finally identify someone whose desires are compatible with yours. Agreement is reached, an exchange completed and you both scurry off, half-guilty, half-satisfied. The whole charmless event is enlivened by the perpetual threat of a militsia swoop and round-up.

10 · Private transport

Because the entire export quota of Soviet cars is snapped up by Progressive countries like Laos and Yemen, British motor enthusiasts may be unfamiliar with models manufactured in the Soviet Union. In common with other foreign cars, these are small, shabby and incapable of cruising at less than sixty miles an hour. They have exotic and dashing names like Zaporozhets* and Volga, but are more easily distinguished thus:

long black ones: these are State-owned limousines for Communist Party dignitaries
short yellow ones: these are official taxis
clean white ones: these are operated by the KGB
drab ugly ones: these are privately owned.

Apart from these minor differences, all Soviet cars look exactly the same – and bear a suspicious resemblance to Italian vehicles. This is because the Soviets suffer the indignity of having their cars built in second-hand car plants, sold off years ago by Fiat. However, any insinuation that their motor industry is not self-sufficient is rejected contemptuously by Soviets, as it is common knowledge in the USSR that the motor car was invented by Vladimir Brodsky in 1884.

SECTION ONE: TAXIS

There are certain factors, unique to the classless society that is the Soviet Union, which affect the operation of the taxi service:

1 Russians are always slow to assimilate new ideas where it does not suit them. For example, there is no particular notion of the taxi

* *Zaporozhets*   Cossack from the Zaporozhe region. Bold fearless fighter, and traditional staunch ally of forces of reaction (Khans, Tsars, Führers, etc.).

as public utility – least of all among taxi drivers. To the taxi driver, his cab is his castle – a treasured and zealously-guarded possession. Aggressive gestures from the roadside may cause him to take umbrage.

2 Quite frankly, sometimes the driver has more important business to attend to than pandering to the whims of members of the public . . .

Note the reaction of Soviets, who express no surprise as taxi after empty taxi speeds past in a streak of yellow. Soviets are taught from an early age to 'respect the work of others' and would not dream of imposing themselves on a reluctant cabby.

However, with a certain amount of tact and patience, and the correct technique, it is sometimes possible to stop a taxi.

How *not* to stop a taxi

1 Place one foot in road, slightly raise umbrella, mutter 'Texi' in best Belgravia accent.
Notes Uniquely English approach, long known to be totally ineffectual anywhere else in the world. Your reserve forbids you to raise your voice in public, and your dignity to make any gesture which might be interpreted as a demonstrative request for transportation. The Soviet taxi driver will probably not even notice you, as he skilfully contrives to crush your outstretched foot anyway.

2 Stand in middle of road, flailing arms urgently. Rap politely on windscreen as you are carried away on bonnet.
Notes Continental matador approach. The passenger hopes to psyche out the driver with the old 'whites of eyes' ploy. Mostly effective abroad, as even Italian drivers will generally realize that needless slaughter of pedestrians will lead to exorbitant insurance premiums next time round.

Do not count on such a rational reaction from his Soviet counterpart, as planning for the future is regarded as largely redundant in a country with only nuclear war or Communism to look forward to.

How to stop a taxi

At a safe remove from the roadside, affecting an air of casual confidence, gesture indifferently as the taxi approaches. Do not even look up to see if your signal has been acknowledged. The driver's curiosity has been aroused and he will stop.

Of course, unashamedly waving a large wad of dollars will have the same effect, but is, the authors feel, just a shade too forthright about the true state of the East European economy.

Which taxi to stop

A green light indicates that the taxi is empty, but does not necessarily imply that the driver is unhappy with this arrangement. There is no need to confine your attentions to such vehicles, however, as drivers of occupied cabs will be quite prepared to renegotiate terms with existing passengers to include you.

What to do once the taxi has stopped

At this point the process begins to get a little unfamiliar . . . We in the West have a rather blinkered and limited conception of the taxi, tending to regard it as a public service vehicle which transports passengers from place to place at an exorbitant rate. Soviet taxi drivers, however, are not satisfied with the restricted role of a State-owned conveyance. Impelled by a strong sense of duty towards the community, and a cunning nose for profit, they have branched out into beneficial entrepreneurial ventures, and now offer a whole range of commercial and financial services:

(a) Cabbies are the salvation of the alcoholic caught short by drink shops' early curfew, cruising the streets like a mobile off-licence and selling after-hours vodka at twice the normal retail price.

(b) Offering more flexible hours and a better rate than the State currency exchange office in your hotel, taxi drivers are a boon to the tourist wishing to buy into roubles.

(c) For his passengers' convenience, the driver is prepared to act as commodity broker, trading in all sorts of paraphernalia (cosmetics, jewellery, albums recorded live at Castle Donington, etc.).

(d) As he meets lots of people in his line of work, the cabby is ideally placed to act as a modern-day matchmaker, the intermediary who fixes up alliances between gullible Westerners and gold-digging Soviets with a taste for foreign travel. He takes his commission in roubles now, dollars upon completion.

Amongst these more profitable ventures, *ferrying passengers* is now merely one of the cabby's tax-write-off sidelines. Although taxis do still discharge this ceremonial function, the driver is bound to be disappointed and irritable if it turns out that you are just trying to bum a lift somewhere.

Stating your destination

With so many other concerns on the go, the taxi driver has to be very selective about which fares he accepts. Every application to ride is carefully vetted. The driver does a cost-benefit analysis in his head, plotting the potential profit against how far it takes him out of his way.

Taxi drivers are generally pretty canny about profit margins. They know a fast buck when a walletful flags them down and, when they feel it's worth their while, are prepared to be flexible and take you where you want to go.

It may happen, however, that the feasibility study's findings go the other way: you are deemed an 'uneconomic fare'. In such cases, the driver shakes his head and drives off, leaving you standing awkwardly in the middle of the street.

The journey

With sub-zero temperatures and Soviet workmanship, it is a wonder that cars move at all in Russia. In fact, they do . . . extremely fast, as it happens. Soviet streets give an impression of absolute chaos – not unlike the scenes inside a Soviet shop when several deficit items are sold off simultaneously.

This is due to several factors:

- the almost complete absence of motor vehicles, thanks to the abolition of the bourgeoisie and private transport at a stroke in 1917;
- all Soviet streets are at least six lanes wide, having originally been designed in Tsarist times to accommodate cavalry charges on protesting workers;
- the matching billiard-ball finish of black ice and Soviet tyres; once a car has started moving, only entropy or impact can stop it.

Given this, it is hardly surprising that Soviet drivers have developed habits which appear rather rash to the more sedate British motorist, coached in discipline and self-restraint by long years' exposure to the Great British Bottleneck. Soviet drivers

display a deep indifference to temporal phenomena such as traffic*
regulations and mortality, using:

(*a*) horn instead of brakes at intersections;
(*b*) hand brake instead of steering wheel at right turns.

In addition to this, like his metered brethren in other countries,
the Soviet taxi driver spends a great deal of his time making
unofficial attempts on the World Stock Car Land Speed Record –
and, if you are lucky, you will be invited to share this harrowing
experience with him. A ride like this is particularly therapeutic for
those who find that the heavy Russian diet makes them constipated.

In between negotiating this hostile environment, careering in and
out of lanes, etc., the cabby asks you to consider the following in-
flight services:

- to purchase at competitive rates your evening's supply of vodka;
- to acquire a Soviet spouse from his immediate family;
- to accompany him to an undisclosed location to meet his friend
  Vasya who has a job-lot of Tsarist banknotes on special offer;
- to exchange the contents of your suitcase for his morning's
  takings.

Don't worry if your grasp of the language is insufficient to allow
you to appreciate the finer points of his generous suggestions.
Russian has a convenient expletive, *nyet*, which should cover any
eventuality.

Going the scenic route:

The driver understands that your request to be taken to the
Leningradski Station and step on it may well be blinkered by a
stranger's lack of imagination and experience. He feels that, as a
proud and conscientious citizen, he has a duty to broaden your
outlook. He may, therefore, arrange for you an impromptu mystery
tour of the city, taking in the Museum of Urban Sculpture, several
interesting outlying regions and the street where he lived as a boy,
picking up and offloading passengers, friends and consignments of
ikons along the way.

Do not be surprised by this: the Russians are a very sentimental

---

* If the driver mentions 'traffic', he is doubtless referring to the day's
turnover in ikons and hashish.

people, prone to sudden tugs of nostalgia and impulsive urges to render a service to a foreign visitor. Bear this in mind when settling up: don't forget to subtract fifty kopecks from the amount displayed on the meter for every unwarranted stop-off. The driver's conscience will not allow him to argue; besides, he will certainly have earned enough on the various dodgy investments he has attended to in the course of his journey to cover his losses.

Payment

When your journey ends, you will notice that the *meter* is in one of three states:

(*a*) *Off*　Taxi drivers are deeply suspicious of the meter – the so-called 'spy in the cab'. They feel it hampers their generosity towards a friend for whom they want to do a special deal, and thus they may switch it off entirely, to create a mood of intimacy.

When he drops you at your destination, the cabby will not charge you a precise fee. Rather, he will leave it up to you, saying *skolko vy khotitye* ('as much as you wish'). This is not a generous deferral to your judgement, allowing you to remunerate him in accordance with the quality of the service . . . It is just that, as Soviet taxis are quite cheap by Western standards, he is hoping that in your ignorance you will pay him at the Western, highly inflated, rate.

(*b*) *On*　Should the meter be on, the driver expects a large gratuity on top of whatever paltry sum it indicates – as compensation for all the time taken off from marketeering.

Don't omit to make note of exactly how much any transit passengers pay to the driver and to deduct this from your final bill. Amidst all the excitement, the driver sometimes finds that minor issues, like the moral implications of charging twice for the same service, slip his mind.

(*c*) *Stuck at 5 roubles 42 kopecks*　This figure remains on the meter throughout the day, regardless of fares. It is totally unconnected with the amount you pay cash-in-hand, banked directly by the cabby. Its only relevance is as an approximation of the financial benefit the State derives from the driver's day's work.

Tipping

A leading guidebook on the Soviet Union states that 'tipping is not usual'. Presumably, in the experience of the compilers of that book, walking away from taxis with all limbs intact is also not usual.

SECTION TWO: PRIVATE VEHICLES

Privately-owned vehicles

Cars are expensive in the Soviet Union and, to discourage doomed acquisitive urges, the process of obtaining one is made impossibly wearisome. Very few people actually own a car – because very few people have three years to kill, an uncle in a position of influence, and 10,000 roubles in ready cash.

In view of the exorbitant cash lay-out required to purchase his vehicle, not to mention all the attendant toadying and bribing, those privileged to own one expect some return on the investment. So it is that the few who own their own wheels hire themselves out as an unofficial cut-price minicab service.

State-owned vehicles

As taxis have gone wholesale into duty-free export-import trading, and as few people have the requisite qualifications for acquiring their own, drivers of other vehicles have obligingly filled the gap in the market. Cruising is, therefore, an important pastime – though it is not motivated primarily by machismo as in the United States. En route to assignments, drivers of supply vans and container lorries are always willing to supplement their cargo with human freight.

How to stop a private vehicle

1 Just hail any passing vehicle (fruit lorry, GosTelRadio sound recording equipment van, etc.) with any one of the small range of non-obscene gestures tolerated in the Soviet Union. State your destination, and negotiate a fixed, non-subsequently-renegotiable price for the journey. Shove over the plumbing tools/crates of cabbage, and make yourself comfortable.

Two roubles is normally a perfectly adequate incentive to persuade the driver that he is going where you are going, especially as he probably wasn't going anywhere in particular anyway.

2 Go up to any parked car whose driver is relaxing within. Tap

politely at the window to rouse him from his indolence, and tell him where you want to go.

You will need to use all your powers of persuasion. The Soviet's habitual eagerness to make a profit can always be quelled by the agreeable sensation of sitting around doing nothing – especially if by this simple inaction he can inconvenience someone else.

Do not be put off by his firm refusal. 'Five roubles' is a password with instant transforming power.

You may initially find the practice of haggling both unfamiliar and embarrassing. The English retain the peculiar idea that somehow human dignity and cash-in-hand are mutually exclusive concepts. Soviet society, bowing to the inalienable laws of economics, has long accepted the fact that every man has his price.

3 Occasionally, when there is a crowd of people all frantically hailing private transport, the driver simply halts nearby and puts out an invitation to tender. It is the highest bidder, rather than the first to reach the car, who wins.

Note The Western charitable institution of *hitch-hiking*, based on the liberal precept that it is immoral, and quite possibly illegal, to charge someone money to take them somewhere you are already going anyway, has no place in Soviet society.

Other vehicles

Practically any car can be stopped, hired – possibly even bought outright. There is an unofficial taxi for every occasion:

- should your party be numerous, you can commandeer a minibus between assignments for a modest three roubles;
- those who wish to travel in style and comfort should make financial advances to the chauffeur of a parked VIP limousine.*

However, even in a society as progressive as the Soviet Union, there are certain enforced restrictions on the individual's freedom. You should not solicit or accept lifts from the following:

- militsia car;
- Politburo limousine;

* There is no question of the chauffeur feeling that moonlighting is beneath his dignity, unless his master holds rank above Regional Party Secretary, in which case he will be too frightened.

- KGB Stoogemobile;
- military convoy.

Should you inadvertently hail any of the above classes of vehicle, try to convince the driver that you were just saluting/tugging your forelock: the spontaneous reaction of the conscientious citizen to authority.

Taboo vehicles

By far the most dangerous of these are the *Politburo limousines*, which prey on unwary tourists in Red Square. With the minimum of warning they streak out through the Kremlin gates, reaching speeds of up to seventy miles an hour as they tear across Red Square, mowing down class enemies who have lingered too long over their snapshots of St Basil's Cathedral.

These vehicles are fitted with the conveniences required by senior Communist Party officials: TV, cocktail cabinet, and full cryogenic storage equipment. Their resemblance to hearses is not fortuitous, as one never knows which journey will be the minister's last.

The other type of vehicle worthy of note is the incongruously sparkling white *KGB undercover operations vehicle*, maintained by overly sycophantic subordinates.

Should you wish to familiarize yourself more thoroughly with the work of the internal security services of the USSR, simply hire a private car from your hotel. You will be provided with a courtesy escort of dazzlingly conspicuous white Ladas, which you may observe at your convenience.

11 · Invitation to a Soviet's flat

In comparison with the British, Soviets are recklessly hospitable to foreigners. You are accosted in the street by a stranger. A few mild pleasantries are exchanged. And then – without so much as a five-year preliminary acquaintanceship and a thorough vetting of background, prospects, etc. – you are summarily invited back to his flat. When you arrive, you are not fobbed off with a single glass of sherry and sent on your way as soon as possible. Instead, in honour of his 'esteemed guest', you are treated to a feast of food and drink which must have set the family back half its monthly income.

This appears ludicrous to the British, who, while consenting to furnish gruff directions to a foreigner lost in the street, would never be so rash as to invite him to be a guest at home. Naively, Soviets feel they must remain true to their word; they do not understand that you can easily get away with no more than a 'We really *must* have lunch' – a commitment so vague and blatantly insincere that neither party feels obliged to honour it.

Getting there

The Soviet authorities look askance at the impetuous generosity of their citizenry; perhaps they fear that the country's GNP will be squandered on greedy foreigners taking advantage of the Russians' excessively hospitable nature . . . Through a policy of caution and intimidation, they try to ensure that unofficial meetings between Soviets and foreign nationals are kept to a minimum.

Thus, when going to visit Soviets at their homes:

(a) *Observe punctuality*   After waiting in vain for ten minutes, Soviets are liable to conclude that their foreign guest has been picked up for preliminary questioning, and that a more official visit is to be expected soon. Punctual arrival spares your hosts the unnecessary panic of flushing papers down the toilet and shoving valuable books into the incinerator.

(*b*) *Do not draw attention to yourself* Loud deliberation in English up corridors and staircases may alert other residents in the apartment block. This may turn out to be their long-awaited opportunity to denounce their neighbours, in the hope of pillaging the flat next door when its occupants take up their new residence in Kamchatka.

Bringing a gift

One of the greatest evils of Capitalism is that it panders to the tastes of American tourists and gullible teenagers, and encourages the production of vast quantities of Oxford University baseball caps and T-shirts sporting gruesome pop stars. Due to the inherent puritan-ism of Soviet society, the economy has not yet diversified into total superfluousness and limits itself to the manufacture of functional* goods.

This means that you can amaze your hosts with the full range of Western gimmickry, bought wholesale from the joke shop: whoopee cushions, plastic doggy doos, etc. This prize will immediately be put on display, and may, with years, become a family heirloom, with future generations of Soviets cherishing this fitting symbol of the Western world.

You may feel awkward about fobbing off your Soviet hosts with such useless, tacky items. Soviets, however, know how to respond appropriately – by offering you nasty, tacky items in return. To further Anglo-Soviet understanding, they will give you presents of an educational bent: badges of cities you've never heard of, guidebooks entitled *Industrial Kazakhstan* in the original language, a fortune in Ukrainian hand-painted wooden spoons. In fact, it may at times seem as though International Friendship is just an excuse for offloading on to you crateloads of redundant impedimenta churned out by factories to fulfil production norms.

Note The Soviet economy *has* evolved over the last ten years. *Chewing gum* is no longer the basic monetary unit in such cultural exchanges, but has been supplanted in this role by *Durex*. Whether the Soviets believe that the latter is merely a more sophisticated version of the former is debatable.

* But not necessarily function*ing*.

Preliminary conversation

(*a*) *When you don't have a language in common*   The language barrier and the sensitive/restricted nature of most non-cultural topics usually necessitates that the conversation be replaced by a sort of expedient *name-dropping*. This party game is a hybrid of Snap! and Botticelli. The Soviet rummages around his memory, amidst the vestiges of his limited exposure to Western culture, and tosses out authors, books, literary fragments . . . These consist of the following:

1 classical writers and their texts; [NB: 'Their texts' will be understood in a wider cultural context, and interpreted to cover any text written in vaguely the same historical period.]
'Dickens? *Forsyte Saga*? Burns?'
2 authors who are all but suppressed in the West for their searing indictments of the Establishment;
'O. Henry? James Aldridge? Melvyn Bragg?'

The tourist then tries to think up a polite response and is struck dumb. Despite all our freedom to walk through an uncensored bookshop, the sad fact is that we remain smugly ignorant. Our knowledge of Russian literature is confined to:

1 nineteenth-century novels serialized on the BBC;
'. . . Tolstoy? . . . ?'
2 Soviet apostates whose anti-Communist fulminations are highly valued in the West.
'. . . Solzhenitsyn? . . .'

The conversation goes on to explore *other* areas of world culture – music, sport, etc.

The strange fact that emerges from this ritual exchange is that the only Russians that we have ever heard of are those who are now considered a disgrace to their nation (e.g. Stalin, Trotsky, Dr Sakharov). Correspondingly, those names with which the Russians will eagerly shower you are of Britons who have subsequently been disowned by their homeland (Deep Purple, Rod Stewart, Led Zeppelin).

Once the limited potential of this exercise has been exhausted, the Soviet will try to draw you into a spate of *place-dropping*. This satisfies both parties. The Soviet gets a chance to fantasize about all those cities which he, for politico-economic reasons, is debarred from visiting. You, on the other hand, have occasion to boast unashamedly about how well-travelled you are.

The Soviet rounds off this nodule of conversation with wistful sighs about his home town, and expects you to imitate his rapture. Soviets love their home town; never having travelled anywhere else, they are convinced that it is 'the most beautiful town in the world'. There is something intensely moving about the power of such faith in the face of all reason.

Preliminary conversation

(b) *When you do have a language in common*   Remember, the Russian weather is not variable enough to foster healthy polemic, so you are forced into exchanging views on ideological matters.

In true Marxist fashion, your hosts look upon you as a product of socio-economic determinism. This explains why they open the conversation by asking you point-blank about the size of your salary and living quarters.

However accustomed to Soviet prying you may be by now, you are doubtless flummoxed by the impertinence of such questions. After all, you do not impart the full extent of your executive income even to the Inland Revenue. Do not take umbrage. Soviets do not consider such data personal. They are just doing their own comparative statistical analysis of the respective economies of East and West – and becoming increasingly anxious at the results.

To follow up their market research, your hosts ask you about their own particular social sub-group:

'How much does a teacher/engineer/industrial pump production supervisor earn in England?'

Such a question usually throws the British guest into a panic, simply because half the respected posts in the Soviet Union just don't exist in Britain. Should your interlocutor happen to be an agronomist/meliorator/energeticist, keep him happy by replying with a suitably mean pittance.

There will follow a general political debriefing, in which your host fires at you questions about all aspects of life in the West:

- What about the unemployed who starve?
- Why do you abandon the infirm to die if they can't afford medical care?
- How many children work as chimney sweeps?

Out of courtesy, you should not disconcert your hosts with troubling alternative versions of Western reality, by pointing out, for example, that we *do* have free medical care.* For the Soviet, the purpose of this question-and-answer session is *not* to gain a challenging new perspective, or even to find out the truth. What he seeks is confirmation of what he knows already. If your version does not tally sufficiently with his, he may begin to doubt your veracity.

There is no room for wishy-washy liberal compromise here. The Soviet enquirer does *not* wish to be supplied with a résumé of the pros and cons of a free economy, a judicious appraisal of the individual merits of Socialism and Capitalism. When he challenges you on some issue, he expects:

either   *brazen resistance*, to the tune of some suitably jingoistic rhetoric; he won't *believe* your tales of spin-driers and holidays in the South of France, but will take comfort from the fact that, as you are inventing such outrageous lies, you clearly must have something to hide;
or   *complete capitulation*, a grovelling admission of the all-round superiority of a Marxist state; in which case, he will grin and feel absurdly smug about the paltry mod. cons in his flat.

Try at least to be *committed*: remember, your Soviet has no wish to hear of a world in which there is *no* one absolutely just, viable system.

If you persist in your shilly-shallying, he will test your powers of abstraction to the full, with the plaintive puppy-dog question: 'Is life better here or in the West?' – an issue on which a one-word ruling is required.

Soviets' impression of England

When talking to an ordinary Soviet, you will be struck by his strangely outmoded view of England – a country suffering from the ravages of mass industrialization, the fifteen-hour working day and smallpox epidemics. This picture is based on the word of the two great authorities on contemporary Britain:

(*a*) *Dickens*   In the absence of a literary update, Soviets presume that the workhouses and dark satanic mills are still flourishing†.

---

* At time of going to press there was still a National Health Service in Britain.
† These Dickensian themes are reinforced by the contemporary British fiction published by *Gosizdat* (State Publishing House) – stirring tales of the Cumbrian peasantry uprooted from the soil by the dual evils of industrialization and militarism, revealing the author's hankering for a simple life working the land (e.g. *The Hired Man*, by Melvyn Bragg, Progress Publishing, Moscow, 1979, 1 rouble 60).

(b) *V. I. Lenin*   Lenin lived in London during 1902–3. In a popular scenario, he wandered from the sweatshops of Stepney to the smoking-rooms of Mayfair, muttering in English between clenched teeth 'two nations'. This aphorism has become so celebrated that the Soviet press is reluctant to undermine its universal validity by considering the possibility of change during the intervening eighty-five years.

These traditional views are encouraged by the State as part of a deliberate policy of protection towards its people. The efforts exerted in unstinting struggle against all forms of oppression and exploitation, on behalf of all nations suffering under the yoke of imperialism, leaves the Soviet proletariat exhausted, and prone to sudden losses of self-confidence. To bolster up the nation, the authorities have constructed a comforting tissue of half-truths and distortions about life in the West, sparing the Soviet People those facts likely to cause it distress (large salaries, video recorders, etc.).

Drinking vodka

At this stage, you will be invited to table to engage in the traditional ritual of Soviet hospitality.

The drinking process itself is strictly institutionalized in the Soviet Union. Mixers are forbidden; the only permissible extras to your tumbler of neat vodka are a pickled cucumber and a piece of black bread. Remember that a full glass is an insult to the liver and must be tossed off in one. The procedure for doing this is strict.

(a) Firstly, a toast must be proposed. If you are called upon to do this, use the following rules of thumb:

1 Always toast an abstract (and preferably meaningless) concept.
2 Try to ensure that your toast is synonymous with the previous toast.

Thus, the running order of toasts is usually:

- To our meeting.
- To our acquaintanceship.
- To friendship.
- To brotherhood.
- To peace.
  etc. etc.

(*b*) Fixing the person opposite you solemnly in the eye, you raise your glass to nose height, eat the bread, knock back the vodka in one, and then, in a peculiar version of solvent abuse, sniff the pickled cucumber. It is considered bad form at this stage to give voice to any natural allergic response (e.g. croaking, choking, throwing up).

NB   The practice of hurling one's glass into the fireplace immediately after draining its contents is strictly confined to fond Western dramatizations of Tolstoy novels. If it is not wholly apocryphal, it has at any rate been completely dispensed with in the Soviet Union – as indeed has the fireplace. Any well-intentioned attempts to reinstate such behaviour will be both revisionist and messy.

The use of the rational faculties of the brain is considered an impediment to genuine enjoyment in the USSR, so the first three or four tumblers are knocked back very quickly. This gives you a ten-minute respite before consciousness is doused altogether, during which time you may sit back and savour the pleasant warm glow of the vodka inside you as it eats through your stomach wall.

Further conversation

Once drunk the Russian likes to get down to philosophical issues – possibly because Soviet reality is too dire, and Western reality too speculative, to make for prolonged and uplifting conversation. With a display of romantic histrionics for which you waited in vain on Parisian café terraces, your Soviet slams another bottle down on the table and says: 'Davaitye pofilosofstvuyem' – 'Let's philosophize'. This type of conversation throws the Westerner into considerable confusion:

1   Most of the philosophers mentioned (Marx, Hegel, Schlegel) are totally unread in Britain – not because of political bias but due to differences in national temperament. The Russian outlook has always favoured untenable idealism, qualified by the inevitable ensuing despondency. Any thinker who conceives life to be a rich and joyous experience is considered shallow and confused.
2   In view of the privileges that your enlightened society offers, you are expected to be well acquainted with the works of Nietzsche, Sartre and other writers unpublished in the Soviet Union. Unfortunately, Soviets do not realize how quickly complacent materialism saps spiritual curiosity. They find Jackie Collins a poor substitute.

However, don't be intimidated when your companion peppers his rhetoric with allusions to Plato, Kant and Hegel. The role of these authorities in the conversation is something of an honorary one. Personal opinions have no weight in the Soviet Union; for any opinion to be considered, it must be attributed to some arbitrary widely-vaunted authority, who acts as a kind of sponsor to the cause under discussion. The rest is left to the imagination of the speaker. So do not be surprised if your host's interpretations of Kant appear unorthodox, and way outside the scope of the *Critique of Pure Reason.*

At this point, you are probably too drunk to concentrate, let alone object to the outrageous liberties he is taking with philosophical theories. No matter: the Soviet is just engaging in his fundamental right to sound off, and doesn't care if you are listening or not. So you are free to sit in a daze, wondering where you are, who he is and how you are going to get back to your hotel.

Departure

Soviets could quite happily go on dropping names and tossing off glasses of vodka all night. Fortunately at some stage he realizes that your system, weaned on halves of lager and lime, has fully capitulated to the half-litre of neat vodka you have drunk. Even Soviets have qualms about shouting pretentious nonsense at vegetables, so arrangements are made for your departure.

At the door, your host subjects you to a traditional Russian farewell – five solid minutes' handshakes, bear-hugs and kisses on both cheeks. Then, with his assurances that the Soviet people do not want war, which you are enjoined to convey to the population of Great Britain, you are deposited senseless in a taxi and sent on your way home.

12 · Official Soviets and stooges

The authorities are aware that you, as a tourist, have come on holiday to relax and get away from the cares and problems of everyday life. The last thing you want is to be bored with nit-picking tales of the niggling imperfections in Soviet society, or to be burdened with the company of uncouth and unpatriotic citizens who insist on washing the State's heavy-soil linen in public.

For this reason, your exposure to lowly, untested members of the population – the warm hospitable ones who spontaneously invite you back to their flats – is minimized. Instead, Intourist puts at your disposal officially-recognized persons, whose permanently sunny outlook helps to compensate for the sub-zero climate.

TOURIST CLASS SERVICE

Provided your lifestyle is normal and well-adjusted and exhibits a minimum of imagination (i.e. spending evenings in the foreign currency bar, diligently going on all excursions), the authorities will deem it sufficient to organize for you one evening a 'Meeting with Soviet Youth' at the *House of Friendship*.*

A meeting with 'youth' probably has connotations of one of those chat shows on Channel Four when you are given an opportunity to hear 'young people' speaking out on the only topics that awaken any interest in these gormless casualties of Thatcherism: i.e. drugs, sexual licence, squatters' rights . . .

* *House of Friendship* Worried about the consequences if left in the hands of private enterprise, the concept of friendship has been nationalized in the USSR and assigned its own particular domain – within the four highly-sensitized walls of this building. Visitors are free to drop in any time and relax and unwind with fully paid-up members of the KGB.

A meeting with *Soviet* youth puts you into contact with a different breed of 'young person' altogether. These are upwardly-mobile careerists, who, through hard work, family connections and/or assiduous and unstinting toadying, have risen up the hierarchy to hold high rank in the KomSoMol (Young Communist Organization).

Their view of the world is formed not through personal observation, but from their studies in Scientific Atheism and the History of the Communist Party of the Soviet Union – compulsory subjects in all Soviet universities and the essential attributes of a well-rounded Party cadre. This, along with a life subscription to *Komsomolskaya Pravda,** has tempered their ability to withstand prolonged exposure to foreigners. Indeed very little of their contact with Westerners has rubbed off on them – leaving them totally devoid of sense of dress or humour.

As notions such as independence of thought and action are utterly unconceived among such types, these upstanding young Communists find it impossible to believe that you could have come to the USSR just like that, of your own free will. They assume that you, like they, are in somebody's pocket, and will chuckle at your rich and risqué humour when you claim not to be.

As to the vital question of your political affiliation, the options, as they see them, are these:

either you are a member of an *official delegation* representing some progressive cause (e.g. Camden and Islington Left-Wing Alliance Council of Young Stooges) come to pay sycophantic court to all things Soviet. As you are immediately recognizable in this capacity due to your hectoring preoccupation with Reagan, Thatcher and missiles, the Soviets relax and swap anti-Western denunciations with you.

or you are a *Government propagandist* like themselves, chosen to represent the official line and groomed in all the requisite diplomatic skills (patronizing, blustering, missing the point). Any comment you make will be received as an official pronouncement from the Court of St James, and the Soviets will put themselves on full battle readiness.

* *Komsomolskaya Pravda* (Young Communists' Pravda) If anything, even more turgid than its parent organ. Instructs young people to follow the 'Leninist model of life' and warns of the anarchic and antisocial consequences of alcohol, hooliganism and leisure time.

Upwardly mobile careerists.

With your status now established as the latter, conversation begins and quickly branches out into an International Forum. This is because, like all good patriots, the Soviet has subordinated his personal desires and satisfactions to the common good. The apparent effect of this is that all supposed *common* actions of the Soviet people, past and present, national and international, redound to his *personal* credit. In view of his own miserably unrealized existence, he is more than happy to talk politics, boasting about just about everything the Soviet Union has ever done.

You are expected to respond with an equally categorical profession of faith in your Government and politico-economic system, praising the heroic deeds of the British people under the sage and benevolent leadership of the Conservative Party.

The Soviets are very keen to liberate you from your intellectual servitude and do not like the use of evasion tactics on your part. Beware of claiming exemption from ideological confrontation on the grounds that you are:

(*a*) *Apolitical*   Soviets do not let you get away with the cop-out of claiming that you are not interested in politics. They have a stock of extra special distortions, guaranteed to provoke the most indifferent and placid interlocutor and draw him into open ideological combat.

(*b*) *An individual*   You may protest that you have been bought by neither government, that you are a private citizen who holds but one of 55 million differing opinions in Britain. The Soviets, deeply patriotic and imbued with a collectivist instinct, are sceptical about such rash and irresponsible claims. That a Briton might diverge in his views from those of his Government strikes Soviets as anarchic – indicative of a decadence and volatility that they find hard to believe even of the Western world.

(*c*) *A liberal bore*   In the course of a detailed and balanced overview of world affairs, you may start to criticize certain actions of your own Government. At this the Soviets will become confused and wary – thinking it some elaborate ploy to catch them out. Remember it is much better for both parties if the Soviets continue to believe that you are a quasi-governmental stooge, than if they contemplate the sinister alternative – that you are a member of the USSR internal security services masquerading as a tourist to test their loyalty.

The Soviet activist, primed for a good clean kill, is most happy when faced with a Western 'Defender of Freedom', whose sole purpose in coming to the USSR, is to harangue every available Soviet about the evils of Marxism–Leninism (Afghanistan, Stalin, etc.). He is fresh from his triumph at Khatyn War Memorial Complex, which he mistook for Katyn forest and reduced the guide to tears with his blustering accusations. Having learned nothing from the experience, he now wades straight in with a block-busting tirade on human rights violations.

The Soviet becomes animated as he recognizes in his assailant the same qualities that have brought *him* to where he is today – obduracy, wilful ignorance and slavish sycophancy. However putting aside his professional respect for his opponent, he treats him to an admirable display of casuistry.

Listening carefully to every charge brought against the Soviet state, he responds with a symmetrical accusation of Western governments. Any rebuke made about any aspect of Soviet reality is smugly parried with an identical rebuke about Western life – with a few insults thrown in for good measure. As Napoleon and Hitler learned to their cost, Russians remain steadfast in the face of Western European attack. The *agent provocateur* sent by a hostile imperialist government to upset the fragile edifice of Proletarian Internationalism is met with the tried and tested method of attrition warfare – and is worn down by an extremely tedious tit-for-tat debate.

The discussion may range on unabated for some time, with the only variable being both parties' attitudes to hard fact which becomes more flexible and whimsical as the debate goes on. The smart money, however, is always on the Soviet to take the honours. As there is no common factual ground between the two sides, it is the candidate who can back up his arguments with the most pig-headed bigotry who will triumph. It is a sad indictment on the British educational system, but the Soviet is best equipped to do this, as his view of world events is clear and not cluttered with exposure to alternative interpretations or infiltration of narrow subjective opinion.

If you are wise you will realize in advance that any discussion of the material or spiritual aspects of life on either side of the Iron Curtain will, at the insistence of your Soviet interlocutor, lead to a huge red-faced slanging match. Steering the conversation on to neutral territory is a fairly demanding task when the whole of the human experience is a potential ideological battleground, but you may succeed in uncovering a secret love of the early Elton John catalogue in your partner and in this way submit yourself to an evening of acute but preferential dullness.

Useful expression

Мир! Дружьа!   Mir! Druzhba!   Peace! Friendship!

Essential leitmotif of any conversation between Soviet stooge and Western left-wing militant. Used in lieu of articulate exchange of opinions and ideas on world affairs.

EXECUTIVE CLASS SERVICE

Should you enjoy high rank in British Military Intelligence, or be travelling in a small group and off the beaten track, certain official personnel will be at your disposal in the comfort of your hotel.

The hotel manager   As a mark of respect to his Western visitors, the manager may courteously invite you down to his office for an informal chat. He will then occupy you for half an hour with inane platitudes about nuclear war whilst an army of frenzied stooges tears apart your luggage upstairs. The more astute manager will avail himself of this opportunity to quiz you on your motives for visiting his town – especially if he knows as well as you that this 'beautiful and ancient capital with its wide avenues and numerous industrial products' is a notorious shit-hole.

   His expressions of polite curiosity (which political organizations you belong to, names and addresses of all your Soviet friends) will be abruptly curtailed by a single ring of the telephone, signalling that seismic upheavals in your room have ceased. You are now free to rejoin your reconstituted belongings.

The stooge   This familiar figure of Russian literature, much beloved in the West, traditionally sits in the hotel lobby reading a newspaper with a hole in the middle. He can also be found tortuously tying his shoelaces for long hours while you are talking to a friend. Coincidentally books on the same sightseeing excursion as you. To supplement his miserable Special Service salary, he also moonlights as hotel maintenance man and may be found carrying out checks for structural defects in the outside of the door and walls of your hotel room.

The guest in Room 1   The most influential man in the hotel. He doesn't appear to have a day job, and – from a glance into his room – is clearly into home-taping in a big way. He also has a friend called Boris who is quite quiet. However he is not hostile, secretive and sexually suspect like MI6 agents: he will cordially invite you in for champagne and sodium pentothal and engage you in free and frank conversation about your travelling companions. Often he will even take time to return the visit personally when you are out.

13 · Introduction to Soviet bureaucracy

Useful expression

Нельзя!   Nelzya!   It is forbidden!

Things to do (4): Banya

The Russian public steam bath (*banya*) is a cultural hybrid which borrows freely from the Finnish sauna and the Turkish political detention centre. Despite the painless passport to cleanliness available in most Soviet homes (the bathroom), *banyas* are still widely frequented. To justify this deviant behaviour, Russians claim that a steam bath strengthens the organism, by sweating out any incipient maladies. More cynical observers see in it a manifestation of innate Russian masochism – as exemplified by the Flagellants and other suspect religious sects in the eighteenth century, and by advocates of Marxism–Leninism today.

You buy a ticket for a two hour session, which is about as much as you will be able to stand, and go through to the changing rooms. Suspicious Westerners, having taken off all their clothes, will want to safeguard their valuables (top hat, silver-topped cane, gold watch-fob, etc.). Security lockers are naturally not available, as the hoarding of private property is not in keeping with Socialist norms. Instead, you must entrust your possessions to the attendant. In one of those rare occasions in the Soviet Union where personal initiative is encouraged, the naked bather is then handed a numbered metal token in return . . .

You are also given a 'towel', which is in fact a sheet. It is entirely useless: the first time you try to dry yourself with it, it becomes completely sodden, and from then on it clings in a damp mass around your loins – ensuring that you go through the whole process feeling like an out-take from *Caligula*.

You then pass into the *banya* rooms. To gain maximum benefit from this experience, you should repeat the following sequence until the muscles are firm and toned, or until the onset of natural death.

1 You enter the *steam room*, which contains a huge furnace and rows of wooden benches. As the steam clears, you notice that flabby

clients are lying gut-down on the benches and being subjected to vigorous thrashings with clumps of birch twigs by other bathers. This behaviour is quite normal and need not be reported to the Commission for State Security. It is engaged in for convincing medical reasons: to open the pores and clear away dead skin. It is also an excellent way of passing on hepatitis.

After a few minutes, someone will hand you one of these lethal posies and request to be beaten. Soviets like to go the whole hog where corporal suffering is involved, and will be offended if you don't thrash them to within an inch of their lives. Remember that they will not spare the rod when your turn comes, but will beat you until there are tears in your eyes and state secrets on your lips.

Every *banya* employs a *banshchik*, a corpulent man chosen for his malevolence and ability to endure hell-fire temperatures. He is at the service of the client: obliging those who are holding out against suffocation by throwing more water on the hot coals, and volunteering his expert and particularly vicious services as whipper.

Ideally you should relax – though well-bred English people do not feel entirely at ease in a room full of naked strangers beating one another. Men should avail themselves of the opportunity to discover facts prudishly not revealed by the Museum of Ethnography, by goggling at a few low-slung Armenians, while women may marvel at the dreadnought construction of the *babushka*.

2 Originally, when you could bear the volcanic heat no longer, you raced outside and threw yourself into the nearest snow-drift. In the interests of public decency, you now plunge into a large *pool of iced water*, which is equally unpleasant.

A quick shower lulls your body into a false sense of security before repeating this series of outrages.

3 To reward themselves for their hour's dedication to the creation of body beautiful, Russian men will then treat themselves to a leisurely unwinding in the *banya*'s own *bar*. This is possibly the most macabre vision of all, as the scene of naked corpulence is surveyed with faint disdain by a barman in tuxedo and bow-tie.

The Kremlin's new laws prohibiting the sale of alcohol in public places has only led to the tripling of the cost of drinks touted by the barman. Aware that most customers will be suffering from severe dehydration, he stocks only vodka. Those not wishing to court heart failure usually try to sneak in beer or wine, though the smuggler of bulky goods is at a considerable disadvantage when completely naked.

Bathers are usually feeling a little light-headed by this stage, due to oxygen starvation to the brain and the effects of the vodka, and retire to the showers to spray one another with water before getting dressed. At this stage, the truly democratic nature of the *banya* becomes apparent, as the client who had previously exhibited the most delinquent behaviour in the showers proceeds to don a high-ranking military uniform, leaving one to ponder weightily on the implications . . .

14 · Invitation to a disreputable Soviet's flat

In the course of your stay, you will be accosted in the street by a young Soviet, attracted neither by your superficial Western characteristics (jeans) nor by what lies underneath – but by the abstract quality of Westernness. A Westerner is a good excuse for a party, and you will be carried off immediately like a trophy to be shown off to his friends.

Most young Russians' 'digs' are dingy, poky, backrooms of communal apartments – not, as you romantically assume, because of their Dostoevskian love of squalor, but, more prosaically, due to the housing crisis. You will be shown into one such claustrophobic 'pad'. Crammed into it are eight or ten Soviet bohemians, a pastiche of the different youth fashions of the sixties and seventies. All extra space is taken up by the noxious fumes of Russian cigarettes. The walls are covered in posters of Pink Floyd and The Beatles. The table is cluttered with bottles: vodka for the men, white wine for the women . . .

DRINKING

Whatever time you arrive, they will already have started drinking, so, before being formally introduced, you are obliged to pay a 'fine' for your tardiness. As the currency on such occasions is human debasement, your punishment takes the form of downing a large beaker of neat spirits in one.

Very quickly you are drawn into the familiar routine of toasting an absurd concept and knocking back a glass of vodka. The only variation is that, out of deference to old Russian chivalry, a few patronizing toasts must be offered to the women present.

Toasts

You are already familiar with the sorts of toasts that must be drunk on such occasions. In this particular company you will usually find that the *spirit* of international solidarity soldiers on, long after the imagination has faltered:

1 To our meeting.
2 To our acquaintanceship.
3 To the beautiful ladies.
4 To friendship.
5 To international friendship.
6 To friendship between nations.
     etc. etc.

This is accompanied by impromptu cuisine: a coagulation of onions, mushrooms and potatoes, welded together by sunflower seed oil, topped with sardines and pickled tomatoes, eaten straight out of the frying pan.

WHAT YOU DO

1 Mixed gathering

(*a*) *Conversation* At parties in Britain we tend to talk about material things (cars, holidays, careers) – especially if ours are larger or more successful than those of our interlocutors. Soviets prefer more wistful 'conversation for the soul', and discourse on metaphysical themes of the abstract and unattainable: love, God, life in the West.

(*b*) *Self-entertainment* One of the gathering picks up a guitar and accompanies herself singing a languid Russian folk song, yearning for silver birch forests and the mushroom-picking season. Another, a poet, will declaim angry verses whose presumed seditiousness is undermined by their pretentious, portentous obscurity. A third will add a bit of spice to the evening by telling a few naughty jokes about the Politburo and putting you all at risk of labour camp slavery.

As a Westerner, spiritually connected to John Lennon,* you are expected to come up with a few soulful songs and poems of your

* Though Lenin is the officially designated object of idolatry, it is his English namesake to whom the majority of the population are passionately devoted. A Briton is the sole catalyst required to cause a Russian and an acoustic guitar to interact. The precipitate is an unpleasant rendition of 'Imagine' in the original language.

own. Unfortunately, none of the great musician's gifts have rubbed off on you – your principal party pieces being parking yourself in front of a video recorder or playing Trivial Pursuits.

2 Male-only gathering

A *malchishnik* (boys' night) calls for great feats of laddishness. For some reason, the exclusion of representatives of 50 per cent of the human race from such gatherings necessitates the exclusion of 99 per cent of the human experience from the conversation. The only subject discussed is *alcohol*. Each tells grossly exaggerated stories of getting into fights with militsia officers, being mugged by Georgians and waking up in various picturesque gutters all over the city.

Swearing makes up about half of the active vocabulary on these evenings. Three root words, permuted by prefixes and suffixes, are sufficient to cover the limited experiences in the life of a Russian drinker.

What to do when the drink runs out

In England, the end of the drink signals the end of the evening. Everyone mutters civil regrets about tomorrow being another day, and leaves with consciousness and dignity more or less intact.

Not so with Soviets, who will be extremely offended if you use the temporary shortage of alcohol as an excuse for breaking up their *vesyolaya kompaniya* (merry gathering).

WARNING   *Insist on leaving at this point.* Those who stay on do so *at their own peril.*

(*a*) One of the company is selected to go outside to flag down a mobile off-licence and buy some more *vodka*. The outward-bound leg of this journey is easy enough, as is the purchase itself, thanks to the round-the-clock efficiency of the black economy. Only when you turn to go back do you realize that you have no idea which of the seventeen identical high-rise blocks you emanated from. You must trudge dolefully up to flat 69 of each one in turn until you are finally reunited with your comrades.

(*b*) Resort to the lethal *portvein*.* The dessert wine and laxative *portvein*

---

* Much greater resourcefulness is required of the Soviet wine drinker than the straightforward mastering of the corkscrew. The *cork* has become obsolete in

is the product of a complex petrochemical process, including macrosaccharination, kept secret by order of the Ministry of Defence. Before inflicting this upon yourself, you should be well fortified by other alcohol.

(c) Scour round the flat for *something else to drink*. His instinct for self-preservation eroded by alcohol, the Soviet rummages around refrigerators and cupboards in search of anything remotely liquid. He usually digs out one of the following:

1 *Surgical spirit* Pilfered from laboratories and operating theatres and served neat. When applied externally, numbs one to local pain; internal consumption anaesthetizes the whole body and mind.

2 *Samogon* Home-distilled spirits, renowned for their psychotropic effects and for playing havoc with your eyesight.

3 *Eau de cologne* Rather than absorbing it in small amounts through pores behind the ears as we do in the West, the Russian joy-drinker liberally douses his throat with it. It gives an esoteric thrill *and* refreshes your breath.

Rituals attendant upon the consumption of these drinks are immediately forgotten by the participants, and are thus undocumented.

Toasts (continued)

16 To friendship between . . . our provinces . . . and regions.
17 To . . . whatever we started with.
18 To Sasha . . . why didn't he come?
19 What do we drink to now? . . . just drink.
20 My friend blubber blubber how I love you.
21 Will you give me a little souvenir . . . your digital watch?

By now the room offers scenes of devastation. Andrei is hunched up with the guitar, struggling to perform for your benefit a song called 'Hard-Lovin' Whisky-Drinkin' Woman'. Much to your embarrassment you find this reduces you to blubberings of nostalgia

---

the USSR and been replaced by the more advanced *thick plastic top*. In this case, unfortunately, technology is way in advance of man's capacity to use it. To remove the plastic top, you must *either* burn half of it off *or* hack away at it with a knife. Understandably, this factor militates heavily against wine consumption.

for your motherland. Sergei is lying on the bed completely gaga. Two others have gone out, Captain Oates-like, into the snow in search of vodka, and have not been heard of since. Olga and Katya, who have finally graduated to cognac, look on loftily at this spectacle of machismo brought low.

DRUNKENNESS

The Russian male, when drunk, is distinguished by his state of slobbery idiocy. This is probably due to* the corruptive power of the mass media. In the West, our screens are full of explicit sex and violence; with these images subliminally implanted in our brains, we become lustful and aggressive when we drink. Soviet TV, on the other hand, features turgid Governmental guff about workers' solidarity and the peace-loving internationalist policies of the Soviet Union. So, when Soviets drink, they become absurdly affectionate.

Your behaviour is liable to tend to the other extreme. The preferred beverages of the West (beer, wine) have the useful property of bloating your body at the same time as they dull your mind – so that both are incapacitated at roughly the same rate. To drink half a bottle of vodka in company, by contrast, is the equivalent of having a brain-bypass operation. You are merely relieved of memory and conscience for the evening – retribution on your body is saved until the next morning. Certain behavioural patterns characteristic of this manic state have been discerned, including tendencies to:

- see your whole life pass before you;
- chase your new friends round the flat brandishing a kitchen knife;
- hang from top floor windows of housing estates.

DEPARTURE

Worse than this, you may find that the moronic sentimentality of your Soviet drinking companions has rubbed off on you. In this vacuous state, you will somehow find your way to the nearest Metro station. There, grinning and stumbling along the platform, you will shout a euphoric message of 'peace' to all those representatives of

* *probably due to*   authorial expression to introduce contrived joke.

Progressive Humanity waiting for the last train. This behaviour is so absurdly soulful that even the Russians find it embarrassing, and will deflect your lunging embrace on to a convenient marble pillar.

As you piece together dim memories the next morning, you may become embarrassed and concerned about your ludicrously mawkish behaviour in the latter stages of the evening. The spontaneous appearance of this peculiarly Russian mood under the influence of vodka, may lead you to speculate:

Is it that:

(*a*) Normal Soviet behaviour is so moronic that it is exhibited by *well-adjusted* human beings only after they have been regressed to early childhood by alcohol?

or

(*b*) Westerners are so aggressive and up-tight that they are wholly incapable of spontaneous expression or compassion without artificial relaxants?

Either conclusion augurs badly for the future of the world . . .

15 · Alcoholism

Though quick to extol the record-breaking feats of their gymnasts and steel-workers, the authorities are rather more modest about the Stakhanovite strivings of the Soviet people with regard to vodka consumption. In fact, given its usual love of statistics, the Soviet media are surprisingly reticent about revealing figures on alcohol intake.

Up until recently, the Kremlin has adopted a cautious approach to the proletariat's predilection for alcohol. The retail price of vodka modulates between two extremes: expensive enough so that alcoholism does not reach epidemic proportions, but cheap enough so that the Soviet people are not forced to sit around indulging in sober free thought.

M. S. Gorbachev's arrival at the head of the Party has altered attitudes. He has categorically diagnosed the condition of Soviet economy: with its flagging trade figures and bleary-eyed productivity, it is suffering from chronic alcoholism. On 17 May 1985, a new era in Soviet history began with the publication of the Party's decree: 'Measures for the Overcoming of Drunkenness and Alcoholism'. This radical legislation is aimed not only at reducing the USSR's world-beating alcoholism statistics, but also at the liquidation of the Soviet alcoholic as a class.

In its analysis of the root causes of the problem, the Party has not been swayed by the near-hysterical ravings of trendy Western sociologists, who view alcoholism as a product of various socio-economic factors (lack of financial incentive, despair, meaninglessness, etc.). Instead, it has shrewdly perceived that Soviet adults drink an average of fourteen litres of vodka a year solely because they are thirsty.

Bearing this in mind, it has taken simple and effective measures:

1 suppressing the sale of alcohol – with no warning closing down all off-licences and proclaiming a new age of sobriety;*
2 offering a franchise to Western manufacturers of soft drinks, and glutting the market with thirst-quenching Soviet-produced 'pop'.

This has given a new lease of life to the Soviet alcoholic. Freed from the burden of drinking his way through his disposable income and cultivating blocked arteries, the new-look alky toasts the Party's health with Fanta or Pepsi-Cola, or drowns his sorrows with Buratino lemonade.

A DAY IN THE LIFE OF A SOVIET ALCOHOLIC (OLD STYLE)

Out of nostalgia for the ways of old Russia, or else out of spinelessness, you may succumb to the pressures of your disreputable friends to honour the ancient and soon-to-be-extinct traditions of the Russian alcoholic.

As your initiation rite, you will have to ingest this *time-delay cocktail*, with the following timetable:

11 a.m.–6 p.m. (intermittently)	beer
6 p.m.–9 p.m.	vodka
9 p.m.–midnight	portvein
midnight onwards	samogon, surgical spirit, etc.

Notice that, for the Soviet, alcoholism is a rigorous and all-embracing discipline. Soviet alcoholics do not specialize in one particular branch of the subject (e.g. meths-drinking); they observe strict impartiality, accommodating in their livers *all* types of alcohol, regardless of vintage, colour or toxic properties.

The ingredients are consumed in strict rotation, in decreasing order of chemical complexity: beginning with conventional beverages, and ending with the closest approximation to pure ethanol that the cleaning lady's cupboard can provide.†

* Much the same conclusions are drawn by our own Government in its sage appraisal that the answer to football hooliganism is to ban football – it clearly being the sight of Millwall colours that incites otherwise honest and God-fearing citizens into orgies of lawlessness.
† The evening is often rounded off with a shot of industrial balm (boot polish, axle grease, etc.) with which to soothe the beleaguered stomach – but detailed treatment of this would no doubt upset the reader's delicate disposition, as well as stretch his credulity.

You must consume this peripatetic cocktail in a variety of picturesque locations (dealt with in more detail below). Staggering between these, along with intermittent brawls, ensures that the mixture is shaken not stirred.

Note Women are precluded from participating on grounds of gender. In one of the rare instances of discrimination in Socialist society, excessive drinking is still enshrined as an exclusively male activity. So women are denied the right to:

- spend the night under cold shower in drying-out room at police station;
- sprawl in snow-drift leering at passers-by;
- wrestle under table with Latvians.

With the advent of Communism, this last vestige of patriarchy will be eradicated, and the above privileges will be denied to everybody.

DRINKING OUT

Stage 1 (beginners)

There can be few things less appealing on an icy December morning than a greasy pint of bile-coloured beer. Yet, strangely, *street beer stalls* do thriving business throughout the winter season, rivalling even the ice-cream sellers.

In fact, trade is brisk throughout the year. The Wicked Witch behind the counter runs a smooth operation, barely rinsing used glasses before drawing another pint of swilly, diluted beer. Customers stand around dolefully, quelling their hangovers with a pint of *Zhigulyovskoye** from a chipped mug, inhaling the noxious fumes of an early-afternoon *papirosa*.†

* *Zhigulyovskoye* Loathsome Russian beer.
† *Papirosa* Loathsome Russian cigarette.

Note on smoking We all appreciate that smoking is essentially a stylized way of transferring large amounts of tar to the lungs. The Russians have chosen to understand this rather literally (as is their wont – viz. founding whole society on dodgy book of ideological speculation). With a rare efficiency, the Soviet tobacco industry has honed the whole smoking process down, cutting out all unnecessary intermediaries, such as filters and enjoyment. The end product is the lethal papirosa . . . possibly a little overpriced at 24 kopecks for 20.

Beer is not a native Russian drink, but penetrated the country through the weak Baltic front. CAMRA enthusiasts may be shocked by the Soviets' apparent disrespect for it. Nobody bothers to measure its specific gravity or take note of the brewery; the consignment of beer is not transported in fetishistically labelled kegs, but just pumped directly from an anonymous van, resembling a Dyno-Rod operation. Beer is appreciated mainly for its therapeutic properties: clearing the head from the previous night's session, and lining the stomach for the night ahead.

Bred to expect the cosy open-fire elegance of the traditional English country pub, you may be in for a bit of a surprise: the traditional Soviet city *beer bar* is characterized by its minimalist décor (bare wooden tables and benches), unique odour (beer and rising damp) and friendly clientele (tablefuls of drunken Soviets slumped over litre mugs or lunging at one another).

For a nation used to tackling neat vodka by the tumblerful, the Russians remain appalling susceptible to beer, feeling ludicrously queasy after two or three pints of the stuff. Considering that the local brews are scarcely more alcoholic than rosehip tea, this is rather mysterious. Presumably, once their guts and bladders are full, their brains are used as emergency overflow.

The nasty flat taste of the beer has necessitated the introduction of certain aids to consumption.

1 Before drinking, you should add a little salt to the beer. This not only improves the beer's flavour, but also enhances its emetic properties.

2 As a gastronomic accompaniment, a *nabor* (assortment) is served, consisting of whatever snacks happen to be lying around. A typical *nabor* is:

- *sukhar* — rusk — hardened piece of black bread
- *vobla* — Caspian roach — carcass of ossified fish
- *yaitso* — egg — cold, soft-boiled egg
- *salo* — fat — horrible bit of pork fat

Reports of violence in these beer bars are generally exaggerated. Any *attempted* grievous bodily harm against one's drinking partner usually ends up as *actual* slobbery embrace collapsed on the floor. The overall impression is of a chaotic rough-and-tumble of teetering, swaying, flailing, stumbling drunkenness – rather as if Hal Roach had directed the violent end of a Chelsea–Millwall match.

The greatest risk that you run if you enter one of these establishments is harassment by Russians in their cups. These citizens feel obliged to extend their feats of bungling *physical* incompetence to *conversation* as well. Should you fall victim to this, you will find drunken Russians:

either boringly coherent – slurring a spurious boast about former fame as an athlete/Don Juan/Hero of Socialist Labour;
or boringly incoherent – putting their arms round you, breathing into your face, and grinning.

It is highly dangerous to allow such individuals to persist in their inevitable first impression of you: viz. that you are a Latvian or a Lithuanian. It is a sad fact, but the Russians are secretly jealous of the stylishness and progressive tastes of the Baltic Republics. As Lithuanians are also one of the few Westernized nationalities out of whom it is permissible to kick the shit (even the Vietnamese are a protected species in the USSR), Russians are not slow to give vent to their culture envy.

In such an emergency, the best evidence of your nationality* is a five-pound note waved hypnotically under the nose of your antagonist. This will cause him to retreat; not *graciously*, because you have proved your point, but *pragmatically*, because it will appear to all around that he is engaging in illicit currency transactions.

If you are a blonde woman, the monotony may be relieved by having six or seven sodden Russian men slump insensibly over you during the course of the evening. Otherwise, the outlook is pretty bleak . . . the best you can hope for is an evening spent swapping inane pleasantries (viz. 'Bobby Charlton', 'Margaret Tetcher') with a non-English-speaking Byelorussian in possession of a hand-me-down brain.

Stage 2 (invoice)

The second station on your Via Dolorosa towards degradation is the *ryumochnaya*, or vodka bar.† These are havens for the 'downtrodden and oppressed' of today, and are extremely sordid, housed in cellars

---

* Of course you do not have your passport on you – it has been retained by Intourist for 'safe-keeping' – i.e. so that this valuable identity document will not be damaged, along with the rest of you, in such confrontations.
† The name is derived from the word for 'little glass' (*ryumka*) – though 'short measure' might be a more accurate rendering.

in the more insalubrious parts of town. Despite the concern of Western conservationists, who are anxious about the Soviet inveterate alcoholic's ability to survive outside his natural habitat, the Soviet government is phasing out these establishments as fast as possible.

You should go alone (talking is against the ethos and traditions of the *ryumochnaya*). To blend into your surroundings, you should disguise yourself in scruffy worker's coat and muddy boots. The rest of the clientele seems to consist exclusively of sewage workers, atomic submarine scrubbers and outpatients from tuberculosis clinics. There are no places to sit; instead, clients loiter at stand-up tables, scowling at one another and knocking back measure after measure of neat vodka. You should mutter sullenly into your glass, cursing the serving woman (Witch! Hag! Poison!) or the vodka (Poison! Bitch!), as the one pours you another glass of the other.

An evening in one of these is the nearest you will ever get to understanding why Raskolnikov killed the old woman . . .

DRINKING DOWN AND OUT

Stage 3 (intermediate)

The next stage of your progressive decline requires you to go along to get in your evening's supply of vodka and portvein at the drink shop.

The Party's anti-alcohol measures include legislation restricting the outlets, and reducing the hours, of sale of spirits and hard liquor. The only effect has been to multiply queue-length by a factor of ten, and to increase the level of bustle to almost riot proportions. Despite their common bond (desperate need for alcohol), Soviet alcoholics can become unpleasantly aggressive if forced to wait for several hours in a queue. The three queue system is confusing at the best of times, but reaches alarming levels of chaos when compounded by the tipsiness of the queuing public.

You may notice a second queue of haggard figures clutching string bags full of empty bottles. They are standing in line for the *priomny punkt*, the collection point for empty bottles at the back of the drink shop. In exchange for a dozen empties, drinkers are given the wherewithal to buy a full bottle. This small incentive triggers off amazing bouts of civic responsibility and ecological concern on the part of the ordinary citizen. Half the population can be found clambering around the town on all fours, rummaging through wastebins, in order to do their patriotic duty.

With your bottles safely tucked into your coat pockets, you will need to find somewhere to go and drink.

(a) *Your friend's flat*   This easy option is complicated by occupational hazards. Out of a deep respect for old and cantankerous relatives, Soviets are usually forced to cohabit with them. This total lack of privacy from Great Patriotic War stories and fond Stalinist reminiscences often forces the younger generation to continue their drinking elsewhere.

(b) *Someone else's flat*   Knock on the doors of neighbours, vague acquaintances and complete strangers, and ask if you and your two disreputable-looking friends can sit in their kitchen and swig from your bottle of portvein. This request is complied with more often than you might suppose (i.e. occasionally).

(c) *Any podyezd*   The entrance halls to residence blocks, with their radiators and grimy stone steps, are very popular last resorts for after-hours drinkers.

Stage 4 (advanced)

If you wish to find the Russian soul at its most trenchant and experience that bleakness of vision and search for the absolute with which we intellectuals associate Russia, you should go along to a drink shop just before closing time.

There is an extraordinary panic in the air. Everyone is scuffling and shoving in the queue, all desperate to complete the crucial vodka-purchasing transaction before the seven o'clock curfew. Rheumy-eyed alcoholics short of the readies tramp up and down beside the queue, selling off old family heirlooms for a sufficient pittance to buy one more bottle.

Should you find yourself without a drinking partner, take advantage of this particular ritual for making the acquaintance of people to whom you have not been formally introduced:

(a) *Casual drinking with strangers*   Someone ahead of you in the queue sticks a three-rouble note up on the wall. You follow suit with another. A bronchitic war veteran trumps it with a third. You now have enough money to buy a bottle between three – one of the

cheaper brands, with the unreplaceable tear-off cap. The three of
you retire solemnly with your purchase to the nearest *podyezd* and
drink in turns straight from the bottle, with the following toasts:

- To women, the bitches . . .
- Whores . . .
- Sh*t . . .
- One more, f*** it . . .
- We're all f***ed . . .
- In the mouth . . .
- In the a*se . . .

(*b*) *Serious drinking with strangers*
Preparation: as above.
Toasts: none.
Just drink, look profound, shake your head, hand the bottle on . . .

16 · Departure

To get you safely off Soviet territory and bring his duties to a close as soon as possible, your guide insists on getting you to the airport at least three hours before the scheduled departure – i.e. five hours before take-off. But, considering the dissolute life you have been leading over the last few chapters, you would probably agree that the sooner you are out of harm's way the better.

The currency exchange office would probably be rather suspicious were you to try to convert into sterling hundreds of black-market roubles, so you spend the first couple of hours in an orgy of spending. Fortunately your Soviet friends, with an instinct for being on hand to receive hand-outs, have turned up to see you off. They acquiesce to your offers of buying rounds of champagne at the airport bar, and even agree to take the surplus cash off your hands in readies.

This flamboyant behaviour alerts the *Customs* officials. Waving everyone else through without even a cursory glance at the samovars, XIIth Moscow Festival of Youth & Students Festival tracksuits and other worthless junk all tourists snap up in the Soviet Union, they are poised and free of distractions for when you come through. They search you methodically, tearing through your luggage in search of gold, icons and smuggled dissidents.

You are then passed on to the cadets at *passport control*. This is not dissimilar to your experience on arrival, only, rather than the agent of imperialist counter-revolution, you are now – to their eyes – cast in an even more loathsome role: that of the treacherous and ungrateful Soviet citizen, trying to do a runner on the Motherland. This occasions more tedium as they examine your physiognomy from every angle, searching for resemblances to known dissidents.

Finally you are allowed to board the British Airways 737. You still have to wait for another eternity until Soviet ground control gives permission for this little oasis of British territory to fly off and rejoin the rest.

British Airways obviously receives a massive Government grant to decondition tourists after a period in the Soviet Union. The whole Moscow–London leg is an induction course back into the Free World. Hardly has the plane lifted off than you are besieged with Sunday colour supplements, vitamin-enriched fruit juices and smoked salmon sandwiches with parsley. The stewards and stewardesses engage you in hearty British banter, keeping you up to date with the trivia of British life (football results, pop charts, race riots, etc.). The captain invites you up to the cockpit to view the wonders of Western technology. By the time you fly over Gotland, you are completely readapted to consumerism, and when you land at Heathrow, you've forgotten about your Soviet experience altogether . . .

Bibliography

The following books are recommended by the authors. They are all available from your local bookseller in attractive jackets with lots of backwards 'R's and 'N's on them.

Everyday Russian Life

1 *The Russians*
2 *Life in Russia*
3 *Among the Russians*
4 *How the Russians Live*
5 *Life Among the Russians*
6 *Russia – Life There*
7–12 (inc) *Russians life the of in among* (anag)

Politics, Economics & Sociology

1 *Red Carpet* – The Priviligensia in Soviet Russia
2 *The Hammer and the Scimitar* – The Resurgence of Islamic Fundamentalism in the USSR (1953 to the present day)
3 *Red Double Cross* – Violations of the Helsinki Treaty inside Soviet Russia
4 *The Bear and the Bamboo-tree* – Sino-Soviet relations in the latter half of the twentieth century
5 *In The Red* – A statistico-economic analysis of the factors surrounding the trade deficit in the East European Economy for the period 1968–72
6 *An Alternative Guide to the Soviet Union* – a collection of verse, song and vibes dedicated to peace and harmony among citizens of the world
7 *Red Herring* – The Soviet Trawling Industry since 1934